A Thorn in Their Side

Sarah Bellhouse

Illustrator: Michael Bellhouse

authorHOUSE®

AuthorHouse™ UK
1663 Liberty Drive
Bloomington, IN 47403 USA
www.authorhouse.co.uk
Phone: UK TFN: 0800 0148641 (Toll Free inside the UK)
*   UK Local: (02) 0369 56322 (+44 20 3695 6322 from outside the UK)*

Published by AuthorHouse 02/22/2022

ISBN: 978-1-6655-9646-6 (sc)
ISBN: 978-1-6655-9647-3 (hc)
ISBN: 978-1-6655-9648-0 (e)

Contents

DEDICATION

To Adam, my son and my rock, who kept
me going when I felt like giving up.
To Michael, my son and illustrator, who believed
in me when I didn't believe in myself.
To Dani, my daughter and typist, who worked
so hard to get this book ready.
And to Teddy, our dog, who reminded me
to have fun when I got too serious.

PROLOGUE

THE BEAST IS RELEASED

He was very excited! He'd discovered the find of the century! Archaeologists everywhere would bow down to him. He wouldn't be surprised if he got a medal from Her Majesty, The Queen. He wiped some more dust from the box. He knew that it contained a very ancient evil and a curse to go with it; not that he held with such nonsense, but it was rather fun to think of people, years ago, afraid of things that go bump in the night. He looked at the part he'd just dusted, there was an inscription there. It was in Spanish. His Spanish was a bit rusty and all he could make out was the word inscription and something about vampires, so he read the inscription out loud, however ill advised this may be and despite every fibre of his being telling him not to. He spoke clearly and concisely so as not to get any words wrong.

No leas esta inscripción o el mayor mal que jamás hayas conocido se levantará y nos destruirá a todos.
"Levántate Thorn, rey de los vampiros. Limpia el mundo de todas las cosas buenas. Y da vida eterna al que te salva"

He sat and waited for a moment and, when nothing happened, he let out the deep breath he hadn't known he'd been holding.

Suddenly, the walls started trembling and bright lights were coming from the box. The man was too paralysed with fear to move, but he was also a little curious as to what would happen next, so he waited, which perhaps was a silly thing to do under the circumstances.

The light grew brighter, until he thought he was going to be blinded, and then he heard an almighty CRACK! The box had broken and out of the light stepped a man. No - not a man - a being. He seemed to glide gracefully across the floor. The man was completely mesmerised by this new presence and stood waiting for what seemed like an eternity. And then the entity was in front of him and looked at him quite curiously. Finally, the being spoke. "Thank you, my friend, for releasing me from my prison," a sly smile appeared on the creature's lips, not that the man noticed; he was still too entranced. "And now for your reward," the being continued.

The man was growing excited again, he was going to get a reward for all his hard work. He was still thinking this when he felt a sharp pain in his neck and everything went black!

Chapter 1

A Fairy Comes to Call

<u>Two weeks later</u>

Kelsey Edwards was playing in her back garden with her dolls and she was bored, and at 6 years old that's saying something. She could see her 15 year old brother, in his room, talking on the phone. He was probably talking to that girl next door. She didn't think the girl was Jonathan's girlfriend, but Jonathan did seem to act weird around her. The girl was called Tara and she had a brat of a little brother called Charlie. He was always being mean to her; sticking worms down her neck and making her eat mud pies. And he thought he was so much more grown up than her; he was only 7. Still, if push came to shove, Kelsey knew she'd end up playing his silly games over the summer. Hang on, what was that? She heard a rustling sound coming from the Laurel Bush. Kelsey sighed; it was probably next door's cat. She was about to get back to her dolls when she saw a bright light shining from the bush and, as she looked on in amazement, the light grew closer and closer until it stopped in front of her. She squinted at the light and could almost make out a shape. Then she heard squeaking... this was very strange.

"Hello," Kelsey whispered, not wanting to frighten whatever it was. All she got were two squeaks in response. "I'm sorry, I don't know..." she shook her head, frustrated, when all of a sudden she sneezed. Someone, or something, had just blown dust at her. She was just about to storm off; she thought it was incredibly rude to have dust thrown at you! And she half thought it might be Charlie playing one of his silly jokes, when she saw a creature in the light. No - not a creature - a fairy. She rubbed her eyes, not quite believing what she was seeing. Kelsey believed in fairies, as all 6 year old girls do, but she couldn't believe there was one in her back garden.

"That's better," came a tiny voice. "Now, can you understand me?"

"Yes," Kelsey replied, still a little stunned. "What can I do for you Miss Fairy?"

"My name is Princess Gwendoline from Fairyland and I very much need your help! So, if you could put me in your pocket and take me up to your brother and get the two children from next door, I'd be most grateful."

Kelsey picked the princess up very carefully and put her in her pocket. She had a lot of questions, but something about this fairy princess kept her quiet, as though she knew all would be revealed when she was ready to hear it.

She went up to Jonathan's room and opened the door. Jonathan glared at her. "Don't you ever knock?" he growled.

"Sorry Jon, but something amazing has happened and I have so much to tell you and..." Kelsey blurted out.

"Whoa," Jonathan interrupted. "Slow down and start at the beginning!"

"I think I should just show you instead," and she placed Gwendoline on Jonathan's desk. Now, all Jonathan could see was a ball of light and hear some squeaking, which is not nearly as impressive to a young man of 15 as it is to a silly little girl of 6. Then he sneezed as the fairy dust was thrown over him. When he opened his eyes, he saw Gwendoline and jumped back making a great effort not to scream, because young men of 15 did not scream and his window was open… and Tara might hear.

Gwendoline spoke. "Hello Jonathan. I am Princess Gwendoline from Fairyland and I need yours and Kelsey's help with a matter of great urgency! Please could you call your friends from next door over and we can begin?"

Jonathan picked up the phone, because it didn't occur to him to disobey this beautiful, regal creature. After briefly explaining to Tara that he needed her and Charlie to come over and that all would be revealed when they did, he put the phone down and sat and stared at Gwendoline. He wanted to ask many questions, but felt too inadequate to do so.

Ten minutes later, when Tara and Charlie had arrived and been dusted, Gwendoline began to speak.

"We need your help," she started.

"Who's we?" interrupted Charlie.

"Do not interrupt little boy, all will be revealed in good time."

Kelsey smirked; she loved Charlie getting told off, especially by a fairy princess.

"As I was saying," Gwendoline continued. "The magical community is in danger and needs your help. Two weeks ago, a very dangerous vampire, called Thorn, escaped from his prison. Unfortunately, the man who dug the prison up released him."

"The archaeologist?" Jonathan interrupted. "But that's my dad, he dug up some 'big deal' ancient thing."

"And you have seen your father in the last two weeks, have you?" asked Gwendoline, fearfully.

"Yes, he's working in the basement."

"This is worse than I feared," Gwendoline continued, her voice shaking slightly. "There is only one reason that Thorn would not have killed your father; that would be to turn him into a vampire and his willing slave. Thorn is very powerful and can do a great many things, including mind control, so when you come across him you must be mindful of this."

"C-c-come across him?" stammered Tara. "Why would we come across him?"

"Because it is written that you are the four warriors sent to defeat him."

"But we're just kids!" Kelsey blurted, trying to contain her excitement.

At this, Gwendoline smiled. "You are not just kids, my dear child, you are so much more than that - as you will find out on your journey. There are many lands for you to travel to, each containing a magical amulet that you need to find, which will be placed in the hollow tree in Fairyland. Once you have collected all 16, there is one more to get from the Vampire Kingdom. This will be the most dangerous to get. There will be many obstacles on your journey, including Thorn and, most likely, your father, so beware! Once the final amulet is in the tree, we must read a small incantation, which will imprison Thorn once more. I will not lie to you, this will be a very perilous journey and each of you will find something out about yourself along the way.

For Jonathan, I present this sword; for Tara, this crossbow; for Charlie, this slingshot; and for Kelsey, this pea shooter." The weapons appeared beside them, like magic.

Kelsey picked up the pea shooter, looking disappointed.

Gwendoline smiled at Kelsey. "This pea shooter is very special, for inside are special tranquiliser darts, that always find their mark."

Kelsey nodded and grinned.

"And for all of you," Gwendoline continued. "A stake each, although a stake won't do much against Thorn as he is much more powerful and very different from other vampires, but it will help you if you come across any others. And a satchel, to put any amulets in; as well as a map of where you need to go. You must get some sleep now and I will collect you all at dawn. Peace be with you." And with that she vanished; leaving Jonathan, Tara, Charlie and Kelsey to look on in amazement and wonderment, each one of them sure they wouldn't sleep tonight.

CHAPTER 2

FAIRYLAND

At dawn, Gwendoline arrived at Jonathan's bedroom window. She knocked twice and Jonathan opened it.

"Are you all ready?" she asked.

"As ready as we'll ever be," Jonathan replied as bravely as he could, not wanting to look like a coward in front of Tara.

"Let's go then."

They all climbed out of Jonathan's window and made their way down to the ground. They followed Gwendoline as best they could, although following a magical creature that's no bigger than your thumb, and that is flying, is remarkably difficult. Still, they managed to keep up until they reached the local woods.

Once there, Gwendoline stopped and the children watched as she began to weave her magic. And they couldn't believe their eyes with what they saw. The earth on the ground was shifting and something was pushing its way out of the ground. As the children stared, this thing grew taller and taller until they were standing in front of the tallest tree they had ever seen.

Gwendoline knocked three times on the tree and a door appeared and was opened by another fairy.

"Princess, you're back!" stated this other fairy.

"Obviously, Colin," Gwendoline replied, haughtily.

"Did you find them?" Colin asked, ignoring Gwendoline's rudeness.

"Yes, here they are." Gwendoline pointed to the four children.

"This is them?" Colin asked incredulously. "But they're just babies."

At this, Jonathan retorted angrily. "I am not a baby, I'm 15 years old!"

Colin chuckled. "They're spirited babies though." And to Jonathan he said, "I'm sure in the human world 15 years old is quite grown up, but I am 546 and still considered a child."

"That's because you behave like a child," Gwendoline grinned. "Now, I must take our young warriors to Mother and Father, so we can begin."

The children followed Gwendoline to a beautiful palace in the middle of Fairyland and entered after her. Her parents were sitting on their thrones, deep in discussion, looking very regal indeed. They stopped when Gwendoline walked in.

"Oh Gwen!" the Queen cried as she gave her only daughter a hug. "And you must be the four young warriors come to save us all."

"Yes, your Majesty," the children replied, bowing.

"Right, let's get down to business," the King boomed, or boomed as much as one can when one's only the size of your thumb. He gestured for the children to sit down and, once they had, he continued. "I know our daughter has told you a little about your quest, now I am to tell you the rest. You will be travelling to many lands, with many dangers. The vampire, Thorn, will try to thwart your every attempt to get the amulets, but he is not your only danger. Some of the lands have wonderful creatures in, such as unicorns and elves; other lands have dangerous creatures in, like goblins and giants. And, of course, dragons fly around everywhere. You already have a map, of course, but I will give you a list of the lands you must go to and what order you must go in. Each of you has a special ability, which will become apparent as the quest continues. What your ability will be, I cannot tell you, but it will come to you in times of great need."

"Um, Sir," Jonathan raised his hand. "Princess Gwendoline told us that our father had been turned into a vampire by Thorn. Is there anything we can do to save him?"

The King looked to his daughter.

"The boy's father was the one who released Thorn. He is not dead, so I can only assume he has been turned."

"Then the boy's father deserves to die, putting us all in danger like this!" the King replied angrily.

"I'm sorry your Majesty, but I'm sure he didn't mean to do it, he's not a bad man." Jonathan was practically in tears.

"No, he is just a very foolish and weak man," the King replied, then listened as his wife whispered to him. "However, you are a very strong young man, so I shall help you. On your quest, in Witch Town, there lives a good witch called Ash. He has a spell that can turn a vampire back into a human. This spell can only be used once and you must get all the ingredients correct. If you fail at this, then I am afraid you will have to kill your father. It will not be easy, as I have no doubt he is being made to do Thorn's bidding, so you must be careful. Now, one last thing before you leave here; here is the amulet from our land. You must take great care of it and guard it with your life." He handed the amulet to Jonathan, who was swiftly becoming the leader.

For the first time since they entered the room, the Queen spoke in her soft, lilting voice. "The first place you must go is Santa's Workshop." Kelsey and Charlie looked very excited and, seeing their faces, the Queen added, "Don't get too excited. Even in a nice land like that, there are still dangers. Some of the elves are evil, as are some of the presents, so you must be very careful. You must travel one mile north from this palace until you reach a forest. In the forest, you will see some earth that has been raised slightly. You must tap on this earth three times and another hollow tree will appear before you. Then tap on the tree a further three times and the door will open. Please accept these gifts from us." The Queen presented them with hats, scarves and gloves. "It gets very cold at Santa's Workshop. Good luck to you all and peace be with you."

Realising they'd been dismissed the children went to leave the room, armed with their weapons, satchel and their new gifts. Gwendoline went up to each of the children as they left the room and gave them a kiss, whispering, "Good luck."

The quest had begun.

CHAPTER 3

SANTA'S WORKSHOP

The children arrived at the small mound of earth and Jonathan tapped on the earth three times with his sword. They watched as the tree grew in front of them and then Jonathan tapped on the tree three more times. A door appeared and the children stepped into - what seemed like - a Winter Wonderland.

"Where do we go now?" Tara asked, sounding pensive.

"I think we need to find Santa," Jonathan replied, trying to sound braver than he felt. "He must be good and able to help us."

The children looked around them and gasped. As well as an assortment of little people, that they could only assume were elves, there were also many big, red, jolly folk.

"Now what?" Tara asked, frustrated. "How do we know which Santas are good and which are bad?"

Jonathan looked around him, not sure how to proceed, when Kelsey started jumping up and down in front of him.

"Not now, Kels! I'm trying to think!" he said impatiently.

"But Jon…" she cried, trying to get his attention.

"NOT NOW!" Jonathan snapped.

"Jonathan!" Tara said sharply. "There's no need for that!" leaving Jonathan feeling quite ashamed at having spoken to his little sister in such a manner, but also a little annoyed at having his leadership questioned already.

"Fine, what is it Kels?" he asked grudgingly.

"Look at the belts on the Santas and the elves." Kelsey pointed, excitedly.

Jonathan looked at the belts. They were all very neatly crafted in leather and looked very smart, but he couldn't see anything extraordinary about them.

Then Tara gasped. "Of course!" she exclaimed.

By now, Jonathan was beginning to feel extremely stupid, as obviously everyone else had realised something he hadn't.

"Don't you see?" Tara asked. "Some belts are black and some are white, so that's how we tell the good from the evil."

"Oh yeah!" Jonathan said, wanting to regain leadership. "So we just have to figure out which colour is good and which colour is evil."

Tara looked at him patiently as if waiting for the realisation to dawn on him, which gradually it did. It wasn't that he was stupid, but being a 15 year old young man, he wasn't used to this fantasy world, because 15 year old young men were too grown up for such things.

"Of course!" he practically shouted, making the others jump. "The white belts are for good and the black belts are for evil, so we need to speak to a Santa with a white belt."

As if by magic a Santa appeared before them.

"What are you four doing here?" he asked rather rudely.

The children looked at the colour of his belt and it was white.

"Are you sure white means good?" Kelsey whispered to her brother.

"As sure as I can be about anything." he whispered back and then turned to the Santa. "Um, excuse me, Sir. We have been sent by the King and Queen of Fairyland on a very important mission to find a magical amulet."

"Ssh!" Santa hissed. "Do you want everyone to know what you're up to? Follow me! Quickly!"

The children followed Santa in the deep snow, through the woods, to a little cabin in the clearing.

"Oh, how adorable!" Tara gasped.

"Yes, yes, it's all very nice!" Santa said impatiently. "Get inside!"

Once all the children were in the cabin, Santa turned and looked at them.

"You don't look much like warriors. Oh well, beggars can't be choosers." he said.

"You're being very rude." Jonathan remarked, crossly.

"Yes, well I haven't got time for niceties and neither have you. You boy! Get away from that!" Santa shouted at Charlie who appeared to be very interested in a box on one of the shelves.

"Charlie!" Tara shouted, grabbing her brother. "I'm sorry, Santa, he's just inquisitive."

"Well, maybe you should tell him about curiosity killing the cat!" Santa huffed.

"You were saying?" Jonathan enquired as politely as he could, trying to get Santa back on topic.

"Oh yes, your coming was foretold, as was Thorn's escape. You need to be careful about who you talk to and be quiet when doing your talking, or you could find yourself in even worse danger than you already are." Then, with his warning seemingly out of the way, he said "the amulet you are looking for is in the heart of Santa's Workshop, the toy factory. Many of the elves and toys are evil and will try to thwart your attempts to get the amulet. The amulet will be in a gift box that you must find in order to continue on your quest. The toy factory is north of these woods. Now go, and good luck!" And with that, both Santa and the cabin disappeared.

"Toys aren't evil!" Charlie scoffed.

"Shush Charlie!" Tara interrupted. "Which way is north, Jonathan?" she asked softly.

Jonathan felt a warm glow that Tara was looking to him to lead them. He looked at the map and pointed to a path in the woods. "We go that way," he said.

The children followed the path and as they came to the edge of the woods, they saw the toy factory. Two elves were guarding the doors. Jonathan sighed with frustration. Now what!

"We need a diversion," he said. "But what?"

"I know!" said Tara. "Kelsey can pretend to be really excited about the presents and lure them out of the way. We can then go in and find the amulet."

Jonathan was torn between wanting to keep his sister safe and finding the amulet. As if sensing his discomfort, Kelsey reassured him. "Don't worry about me, Jon. We need to find the amulets and this is my little job."

"Alright," conceded Jonathan. "But scream if you need us."

Jonathan, Tara and Charlie looked on as Kelsey ran up to the elves, squealing excitedly. The elves turned to her and, in trying to usher her away, abandoned their posts. The other three children crept past them, through the doors, and looked in amazement at all the presents.

"How are we supposed to find the box the amulet's in?" Tara gasped. "There are so many of them."

At her voice, all the elves stopped and looked at them.

"Uh oh," Jonathan whispered as the elves, some blue toy soldiers and remote control trucks started advancing on them. "Now what?"

"Hey!" Charlie cried. "There's a really weird looking doll in that box."

Jonathan looked where Charlie was pointing. The box was shut tight, there was no way of knowing what was in it! Unless...

"X-ray vision!" Jonathan and Tara cried, staring at Charlie.

"Charlie." Tara shouted. "We'll hold them off, you look for the box with the amulet!"

"What's an amulet?" Charlie shouted back, as Jonathan swung his sword at one of the toy soldiers.

"A big necklace looking thing!" Tara screamed at her brother, ducking as one of the elves launched themselves at her.

Suddenly, they heard what sounded like a battle cry and some 'white belt' elves, some dolls and remote control planes came running up behind them.

"I'm liking these odds better!" Jonathan shouted, as he and Tara and their new allies fought the evil elves and toys.

The elves launched themselves at each other, the dolls pulled the soldiers' hair and the planes fired missiles at the trucks. Jonathan swung his sword, as Tara fired arrows, at all the evil beings they could see, whilst Charlie scrambled over all the boxes until they heard him shout, "I've found it!" holding the amulet in his hands. Everyone turned to look at Charlie; the evil toys and elves went pale and backed away as Charlie came down from the pile of boxes. The good toys and elves cheered. Tara picked her brother up and gave him a big kiss.

"Eww!" Charlie grumbled, but looked secretly pleased. Jonathan took the amulet off Charlie and put it in the satchel and ruffled Charlie's hair. "Well done, little man," he praised; feeling quite proud that they had found their first amulet. "And thank you all," he said to the elves and the toys.

The children wandered out of the toy factory and Kelsey came running up to them.

"Have you got it?" she asked breathlessly.

"Yes." Jonathan replied. "What happened to the guard elves?" he asked, looking around, as if expecting them to jump out at him.

"Oh, I outran them," Kelsey shrugged. "They're not very fast, must be all that sitting around."

"Hey look!" Tara pointed at a path in front of them. They all looked and saw a sign to the next land.

"Shall we?" Kelsey gestured.

CHAPTER 4

THE ELF VILLAGE

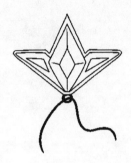

As they walked down the path, they gasped. In front of them was a bustling elfin village; full of beautiful, colourful cottages and many adorable little shops.

"Look!" Kelsey exclaimed as they came to a tiny bakery. "Isn't it cute?"

"Very!" a voice said behind them, making them jump.

They turned to face the voice and saw a small creature, dressed in the most beautifully tailored, lilac clothes standing before them.

"Hello," the creature looked at them. "My name is Simeon, I'm the head good elf. How may I help you?"

The children looked at the elf, unable to speak until Jonathan coughed. "Um, hi. I'm Jonathan and this is my sister, Kelsey and our friends, Charlie and Tara."

Kelsey smirked. Calling Charlie a friend was stretching it a bit, but she said nothing.

"We're searching for something. Can you help us find it?" Jonathan continued, not quite trusting this elf, even though Simeon had assured them he was good.

"Of course," Simeon replied smoothly. "But we must move quickly. My brother, the head bad elf, is on his way over here."

He ushered the children into a small antiques shop next to the bakery. The children looked around the shop, marvelling at all the exquisite antiques for sale.

"Right, now let's get down to business," Simeon stated with an odd look on his face. Jonathan started to speak when he felt Charlie tug on his jacket.

"What is it Charlie?" he asked impatiently, crouching down to listen to him.

"Why is that elf's heart black?" Charlie whispered fearfully, looking directly at Simeon's heart.

Jonathan looked at Simeon, who stood there, looking right back at him.

They stared at each other for a few moments when…

"Run!" Jonathan yelled, and at the same time…

"Get them!" Simeon screeched.

All of a sudden, there were elves everywhere pulling at the children. Some with ropes, tying them up and dragging them to the basement where they locked them in cages, taking their weapons off them and the satchel with the amulets in.

Simeon came down and sneered at the children. "I'm so glad you're here," he smirked. "Thorn will reward me handsomely for delivering you to him."

Hearing the bell from the shop, he went back upstairs, locking the children in the basement.

"What are we going to do now?" cried Tara.

"I don't know!" replied Jonathan gloomily.

"What are they doing up there?" Kelsey asked when they heard a thump and a crash.

The others shrugged. What **was** happening?

There was a scraping and the sound of a bolt opening.

"We must find something to defend ourselves with!" Tara shouted.

The children looked around the cages, but there was nothing but a few stones.

"Right, when that door opens, we pelt them with stones and hopefully one of them will come close enough to grab the keys!" Jonathan ordered.

The others looked at him in despair and he shrugged. "It's the best plan we've got."

The door opened and the children started throwing the stones.

"Hey!" a voice yelled. "Cut it out! Is that any way to treat someone trying to save you?"

The children stopped, amazed and Charlie looked right at the elf. "Yes," he confirmed. "He has a normal heart. He's good."

"Of course I'm good!" the elf spluttered. "I'm Simon, Simeon's brother. Now, if you've finished throwing things at me, may I suggest we leave?"

He unlocked the cages and the children followed him upstairs.

"The amulet you're looking for was in this shop," Simon told them.

"Was?" Tara enquired.

"Yes," came the reply. "In all the fighting, Simeon got away, taking the amulet and all your belongings with him. He hopes to trade them with Thorn for his life. Now, we must hurry!"

The children and Simon hurried out of the shop in pursuit of Simeon. Following Simeon's footsteps, they came to the top of a hill and could see Simeon hurrying down the other side. They were about to follow him when they heard a terrifying screech from above. They looked up and saw flames coming from the sky.

"Dragons!" Simon shouted and pushed the children down the hill.

The children rolled and tumbled down the hill with Simon close behind until they came to a stop at the foot of the hill.

The dragons circled them overhead, shooting fire at them.

"Thorn must have sent them," Simon gasped as he reached them. "We need to get your weapons so we can fight them!"

Jonathan looked at Simon as though he was crazy. Get their weapons? So they can fight the dragons? It was madness!

In amongst the flames and the smoke, they saw a figure approaching them. It was Simeon, looking terrified.

"I don't want to die!" he wept and handed them their weapons, keeping hold of their other belongings.

Jonathan glared at Simeon and he and Tara rushed towards the dragons, brandishing their weapons, hoping against hope that they would prevail.

The biggest, meanest dragon landed in front of them, whilst the rest continued circling. He breathed fire at Jonathan who managed to jump out of the way, just in time.

"We have to get on top of him!" Tara shouted.

Jonathan nodded, looking at the spikes on the dragon's back. They looked like they'd slice a man in half. He ran towards Tara, jumping over the dragon's tail.

"One of us needs to distract him and the other gets on top and stabs him," Jonathan gasped.

Tara nodded. "I'll distract him and you stab him."

"Okay." Jonathan looked at her, stroking her cheek. "Be careful!"

Tara ran underneath the dragon and stabbed him on his big, stomping foot with an arrow. The dragon roared, stomping around in pain, trying to find Tara. Jonathan climbed onto the dragon's tail and made his way up the dragon, when he heard Tara scream.

He looked down and saw the dragon advance towards Tara, who had stumbled and lost her crossbow. He was about to jump down and save her when he saw a smaller dragon approach her. The small dragon nudged Tara and pushed her out of the way, just as the big dragon shot fire at her. Then the small dragon faced the big dragon and shot fire right into his eyes.

The big dragon roared, clawing at his eyes, when Jonathan saw his chance. He scrambled up to the top of the dragon and plunged his sword in hard. The dragon let out a great bellowing roar and reared back. Jonathan lost his balance and fell to the ground, as the dragon toppled over and breathed his last breath. Everyone crowded around Jonathan, who groaned. "Man, I'm going to feel that in the morning!"

Everyone laughed with relief and the small dragon gave him a big lick.

"Well, now that's over, I'll be on my way," Simeon backed away.

"Not so fast!" Jonathan snarled, pointing his sword, which now glistened with the dragon's blood, at Simeon. "Our things!"

"O-o-of course," Simeon stammered. "I wasn't going to keep them!"

"Of course not!" Jonathan looked at him in disgust and grabbed the satchel, and the amulet, swinging from the elf's neck. "Now, get out of here before we lock **you** in a cage!"

Simeon scurried away and Jonathan turned to face the others.

"We need to get back to the shop. I saw the entrance to the next land there and we need to get away from the rest of **them**." He pointed to the rest of the dragons.

The children ran as fast as they could into the village, trying to put as much distance as they could between them and the dragons. The screeching seemed further away and they looked back. The dragons hadn't followed them, but Simeon's friends had and were closing in on them.

The children backed up to Simeon's shop when the small dragon came bounding up to them. He took one look at the menacing elves and shot a small spark of fire at them. The children laughed as the elves hopped around, trying to put themselves out.

Jonathan opened the door and everyone ran into the shop and down to the basement.

"Spread out! It's in here somewhere!" Jonathan insisted. So everyone looked around for the doorway, but no one could find it.

"Hey, what's this?" Charlie suddenly shouted, pulling at a lever.

The others stared at him as the wall behind him opened up. They could hear the elves coming down the stairs and rushed to go through the doorway. The last thing they saw before the wall started to close was Simon preparing to fight the evil army of elves. With one last blast of fire, the small dragon blew them back and the wall closed leaving the angry elves behind.

CHAPTER 5

UNICORN KINGDOM

The children sat on the grass, trying to catch their breath.

"Good boy!" Kelsey fussed over the small dragon.

"Kels!" Jonathan warned.

"We've got to bring him with us; he helped us." Kelsey begged.

Jonathan looked at the three expectant faces before him and groaned. "Alright! But you're in charge of him and you'd better think of a name for him."

Kelsey and Charlie whooped and Tara just smiled. Jonathan had a kind heart, she knew.

"How about we call him Draco?" Tara offered. "It's Latin for dragon."

Kelsey wrinkled her nose and shook her head. "That's too old and stuffy." She frowned, trying to think of a good name.

"What about Sparks?" Charlie grinned as the dragon licked him.

Kelsey looked at Charlie. That was a pretty good name, but she wished she'd thought of it instead of Charlie.

Seeing the look on Kelsey's face, Jonathan intervened. "Sparks it is then."

"Look, he likes it!" he added as Sparks ran around playfully licking each of them.

Jonathan patted Sparks on the head and got up to have a look around. There were soft, green pastures all around them and beautiful, flowing waterfalls and just ahead of them was a wood with hundreds of trees, full of all the fruit they could name. It wasn't a dark, gloomy wood like you would expect, there was a mysterious light emanating from it.

Jonathan could feel himself being pulled towards the light and the others also seemed helpless to resist. They came to the edge of the woods and a hypnotic being stood before them. They were finally going to meet Thorn.

"Come, my children," Thorn spoke to them. At least they thought he spoke, but his lips didn't appear to move.

"Give me the satchel," he continued, in his soft hypnotic voice.

Jonathan handed the satchel of amulets to Thorn. The vampire then beckoned to Tara, who was also under his spell. Sparks tried to drag her away, but the hypnosis was too strong. Tara reached Thorn and he brushed her hair off her neck and bent his head down. Just as he was about to bite her, there was a huge flash of light and he screamed in pain and anger.

The children looked at him, stunned, seeing him properly for the first time. Next to him was a cowering vampire, who didn't look very pleased to see them.

"Daddy!" Kelsey screamed and started to run towards him.

"Kelsey, NO!" Jonathan grabbed her and held her tightly as she sobbed.

Thorn sneered at them. "Soon I shall know your blood!" he snarled and with a huge bang he vanished, taking with him Jonathan's father.

Jonathan looked to see where the flash of light had come from and before him was the most majestic animal he had ever seen.

"My name's Talia. I'm the head unicorn and I have been sent to help you acquire our amulet."

"What's the point?" Jonathan grumbled. "Thorn's got all the other amulets and we're never going to get them back."

"Not with that attitude you won't!" Talia admonished. "Now, collect all the fruit you need for your journey. Then I must take you to the centre of the Unicorn Kingdom where there lies the secret of the amulet."

The children looked at Talia in awe and, when they had collected all the fruit they could carry, they followed her. When they had been walking for about ten minutes, Talia stopped and looked at Kelsey, who was still crying quietly.

"Hush, dear child. What ails you?"

"My daddy is a vampire and we might never get him back!" Kelsey sobbed harder.

"Kelsey, I'm surprised at you! You are the most positive of all of you. You will find the strength to restore your father." Talia looked at her kindly.

"How did you know my name?" Kelsey asked, surprised, quite forgetting to be upset.

"This is a magic place," was all Talia would say and continued leading them to the centre of the kingdom.

Talia led them to the entrance of a cave and told them, "this is where I must leave you young warriors. Inside is the most ancient of our kind. She will help you find the amulet. You must be aware that she only responds to girls, so the boys must stand back and let the girls talk to her." She turned to leave. "Good luck, children."

The children entered the cave, holding hands, too scared to let go of each other. They walked to the centre of the cave, where they saw the most magnificent golden statue they had ever seen.

"It's very rude to stare!" the statue spoke, startling them.

"I-I-I'm sorry, " stammered Jonathan.

"Not you boy! I wish to speak only with the girls."

Jonathan thought this was rather sexist but, remembering the head unicorn's words, wisely said nothing. Tara and Kelsey stepped forward.

"So, what is it you seek?" the golden unicorn asked.

"Well, if you please ma'am, we're looking for the amulet of this kingdom," Tara told her.

The unicorn looked at her, assessing her, then spoke again. "How do I know your intentions are honourable?"

"I guess you don't," Tara admitted. "But we need to get the amulets before Thorn does."

At the mention of Thorn's name the golden unicorn reared up on her hind legs.

"Thorn!" she boomed. "Just how exactly did he escape his prison?"

Knowing there was no other choice, Tara told the unicorn what had happened. When she reached the part about Jonathan's father, the unicorn shot Jonathan a look of disgust, which he thought was unfair. After all, it wasn't he who had released Thorn.

"Very well!" the unicorn said when Tara had finished her story. "I will allow you to take the mystical amulet from around my neck, if you can answer three questions correctly. Question one will be a question from your world, question two will be a question from my world and question three will be about Thorn himself. You must answer all three questions correctly to get the amulet. Do you understand?"

Tara and Kelsey nodded.

"Question one, from the human world. What is 16 squared?"

Tara and Kelsey looked at each other. Kelsey shook her head. She was only 6, she couldn't possibly know the answer.

Tara found a stick and started working the sum out on the cave floor.

```
16 x      16 x      160 +
10        6         96
-----     -----     -----
160       96        256
-----     -----     -----
```

The unicorn looked at her enquiringly.

"Is the answer 256?" Tara asked, hesitantly.

"That is correct," the unicorn replied. "You must have more faith in your abilities. Question two is about Unicorn Kingdom. What do unicorns eat?"

Kelsey and Tara sat down, deep in thought.

"Well, unicorns are a bit like horses, aren't they?" Kelsey asked.

"Yes," replied Tara. "So, what do horses eat?"

"I know!" Kelsey shouted, startling everyone in the cave.

"Yes little girl?" asked the unicorn.

"Hay and oats and things like that."

"That is mostly correct, although we are partial to the fruits of the trees in the wood." Tara tossed her a juicy apple. "However I shall give it to you."

The girls cheered. Two out of three correct, just one more and they'd have the amulet.

"Last question," the unicorn continued when there was silence in the cave once more. "How can Thorn be killed?"

The girls looked at each other aghast. The fairies had told them that Thorn was no ordinary vampire, so the ordinary methods wouldn't work.

"Okay," Tara whispered. "Let's list all the ways we know a vampire can be killed."

"A stake," Kelsey started.

"Garlic," Tara continued.

"A cross..."

"Bible…"

"Silver bullet…"

"Decapitation…" At Kelsey's blank look Tara explained. "Head being chopped off."

"Oh." Kelsey nodded. "Vampires also don't like fire."

"That's it!" Tara almost shouted, making Kelsey jump. "If you chopped off his head and set him on fire, even Thorn couldn't come back from that!" She looked at the unicorn. "Is that right?"

"That is correct, however the most anyone has been able to do is imprison him as he is too strong and too fast."

"So do we get the amulet?" Jonathan asked impatiently.

Tara glared at him. "I'm sorry Miss Unicorn, but we did answer all your questions correctly."

The unicorn began to speak when a rumbling came from within the cave.

"Earthquake!" Jonathan shouted.

"Not quite," came a smooth voice and Thorn stood before them. "Now, give me the amulet unicorn, or you will know my wrath."

"NO!" bellowed the unicorn in the most fearsome voice and her horn glowed, shooting terrible, ancient magic at Thorn.

"Aaargh!" he screamed as he was thrown against the cave wall.

"Quick!" the unicorn urged. "Get the amulet and go. You will find a door at the back of the cave that will take you where you need to go."

"What about you?" Tara asked, scared.

"My dear child, I'll be fine. I can deal with Thorn. Now GO!"

Tara took the amulet off the unicorn and ran with Charlie, Kelsey and Sparks to the back of the cave.

"Come on Jonathan!" she shouted.

Jonathan had crept up to Thorn and could see the satchel tied to Thorn's waist. He grabbed the satchel just as Thorn grabbed his leg. Tara screamed.

"Here!" Jonathan yelled as he threw the satchel to Tara. "Go! I'll catch you up."

Tara hesitated.

"GO!" Jonathan shouted more urgently.

She ran to the doorway, opened it and disappeared into a fog with the others.

The unicorn watched this go on with interest. This boy was different to human boys she'd encountered before, she must help him. She looked around and saw what she must do. She reared back onto her hind legs and stamped … hard. Everything started shaking and the cave walls started crumbling. Thorn let go of Jonathan's leg and Jonathan ran to the unicorn.

"You must go," she said softly. "It is your destiny to save us all."

"Come with us?" Jonathan pleaded.

"Alas, I cannot." She smiled at him.

"But you'll die!"

"I will have fulfilled my destiny to help the most powerful warriors of all time. Now you must go, or you'll be buried too."

Jonathan hugged the unicorn and ran to the doorway. Taking one last look he ran into the fog to help his friends.

Chapter 6

Pegasus Valley

Jonathan made his way through the fog and collapsed on the ground in Pegasus Valley.

"Jonathan!" Tara shrieked, flinging her arms around him.

Ordinarily, this would have thrilled Jonathan, but all he could think about was that last glimpse of the golden unicorn.

"I'm alright!" he said gruffly.

Noticing they were not alone, he looked up and saw a winged horse.

Now Jonathan, who wasn't very well versed in mythology or fairy tales, assumed this was another unicorn and said as much.

The winged horse smiled at him kindly and told him, "I am no unicorn, young man. I am a pegasus. My name is Percival, but everyone calls me Percy."

Jonathan grunted but Percy, knowing what had just happened, did not take offence. Instead he suggested that they all took a few moments to remember the fallen unicorn.

The children bowed their heads, deep in thought, each of them remembering the beautiful golden unicorn in their own way.

When they had finished, they looked up to see Percy gazing intently at them.

"Now, I am to guide you to the next amulet," Percy told them. "Before I do, however, I must tell you what is expected of you. My friends and I will take you to the desert, where you must find the entrances to the place where the amulet is kept. I'm sorry I can't be more specific than that, but there are certain things you must find out for yourselves. Now, shall we go?"

The children nodded and Percy whistled. Three more pegasi swooped down from the skies and landed before them. The children mounted the pegasi, with Kelsey keeping a very tight hold of Sparks; so he didn't fall off, or worse, sink his claws in the pegasus' back. Then they were flying, high above the countryside. The children looked down, amazed at how small everything looked. The pegasi started their descent, having reached their destination and landed gracefully in the middle of the desert. The children slid down to the ground and looked around them.

"There's nothing here!" Charlie grumbled.

The others murmured in agreement.

Percy looked directly at Charlie and said, "Then **you** must look harder, young man," before calling to the other pegasi and flying off into the sky once more.

"What did he mean by that?" Tara wondered. Jonathan felt as stumped as she looked.

"Isn't it obvious?" Kelsey asked impatiently, making both Jonathan and Tara feel very stupid indeed. They shook their heads.

"Charlie needs to use his x ray vision to find the doorways."

"But there's nothing for him to look through," Tara stated quite sensibly, Jonathan thought.

"Maybe it's invisible!" Kelsey replied, sounding more and more excited.

Jonathan and Tara looked sceptical, but nodded to Charlie, who started looking around. The others all sat down, feeling very hot, with the sun beating down on them. Jonathan got out some fruit, from the Unicorn Kingdom, for them all to enjoy.

"Hey, I see something!" Charlie shouted, making them all jump.

"What do you see, Charlie?" Tara asked.

"There's a place over there," he replied, pointing ahead of him. "It's got trees and waterfalls and animals."

Jonathan, Tara and Kelsey couldn't see anything, but knew that this was a magical place, so anything was possible. They made their way to where Charlie was pointing. "Ow!" Jonathan exclaimed crossly. He'd just walked into an invisible wall.

"This must be it," Tara said as Jonathan scowled and rubbed his head.

"Who goes there?" a sharp voice came from behind the invisible wall.

"It is us!" Jonathan explained. "Jonathan, Tara, Kelsey and Charlie."

"Who?" the voice asked and opened a door in the wall. "Oh, it's you four. Next time, just say it's the four warriors come to save you all. It'll save you time." In front of them was a large, rainbow coloured pegasus.

"Um, okay," Jonathan replied, staring at the strange-looking pegasus.

"I am the guard pegasus, shall we begin?" the guard asked impatiently.

The children nodded and the guard sighed, wondering how these four children would fare against the evil that awaited them.

"My puzzle for you is this: "three friends; Pablo, Edvard and Henri are talking to each other about the art collection of

Leonardo. Pablo says: "Leonardo has at least four paintings of Rembrandt." Edvard says: "No, he has less than four paintings of Rembrandt." "According to me," says Henri, "Leonardo has at least one Rembrandt." My question is this, if you know that only one of the three friends is correct, how many Rembrandts does Leonardo possess? You have five minutes to complete this puzzle." He nodded towards the timer.

Tara and Jonathan sat down to discuss the puzzle, They knew Kelsey and Charlie wouldn't be able to. Jonathan felt sure he wouldn't be much help either, but he thought he'd better try.

"Right," said Tara. "It can't be more than four, because Pablo and Henri would be right." Jonathan nodded.

"Then," Tara continued. "It can't be Henri, who said at least one, because Pablo and Edvard would also be right." Again Jonathan nodded, starting to feel decidedly stupid for not contributing, but he hated puzzles and riddles. They always confused him. Besides which, he didn't want to look stupid in front of Tara, so he kept quiet, knowing she'd work it out faster without him interrupting.

Tara gave him a strange look, but continued. "That means that it has to be Edvard, who said less than four, which means Leonardo has less than one Rembrandt, so he has no Rembrandts. Is that right?" She looked up, expectantly at the guard.

"Well done, my girl! That was correct. He wasn't much use was he?" the guard nodded at Jonathan, who looked embarrassed.

Tara looked at Jonathan, softly. "Maybe not, but he saved me from a dragon, so he has other strengths."

Jonathan blushed. "Let's go to the next door," he said gruffly, not wanting Tara to see how pleased he was with her words.

The guard looked at him knowingly and handed him a blue key. "If you walk ten paces to your right and knock on the wall three times, the next door will open and the captain pegasus will give you your next puzzle."

The children did as instructed and knocked on the wall three times.

"Who is it?" a slightly deeper voice asked.

Jonathan remembered what the guard pegasus had told them. "It's the four warriors come to save you all."

The door opened and a shining, silver pegasus stood before them. "Well, that's a bit pretentious, I must say!"

"But…" Jonathan started, pointing at the guard, who snorted with laughter. Jonathan glared at him and the captain stifled a smile.

"For this puzzle, you will be given 8 minutes. Are you ready?"

The children nodded and he continued. "A man has a wolf, a goat and a cabbage. He must cross a river with the two animals and the cabbage. There is a small rowing boat, in which he can take only one thing with him at a time. If, however, the wolf and the goat are left alone, the wolf will eat the goat. If the goat and the cabbage are left alone, the goat will eat the cabbage. How can the man get across the river with the two animals and the cabbage?" He looked at them expectantly.

Jonathan looked back in despair; they were never going to get all the amulets at this rate.

Tara sat down again. Apparently she worked better when she was sitting down, Jonathan thought.

She sighed, deep in thought. "I've got it … oh, no, that wouldn't work. What about…? No, the wolf would eat the goat, so that won't work." She continued like this for 5 minutes, while Jonathan, Kelsey and Charlie looked at the timer going down, then she stood up suddenly.

"I've got it!" she shouted.

The captain and the other children looked at her, waiting.

"First, the man takes the goat across, leaving the wolf with the cabbage. Then he goes back. Next, he takes the wolf across. Then the man goes back, taking the goat with him. After this, he takes the cabbage across, leaving the goat behind. Then he goes back again, leaving the wolf with the cabbage. Finally, he goes back for the goat and takes it across." She beamed proudly.

"Congratulations," the captain said. "You really are a very bright young lady." Tara blushed at this.

"Here is your second key." He handed them a yellow key. "Now you must walk ten paces to the left, twenty paces to the right, five steps back and ten steps forward."

Jonathan looked confused. "But if we only go five steps back, won't we bump into the wall if we try and walk ten steps forward?"

The captain smiled and shook his head. "Have you not learned yet, young man? This is a magical place." With that cryptic message he retreated into the oasis once more.

"Right!" said Jonathan. "Let's go!"

So they walked ten steps to the left, twenty steps to the right, five steps back and started to walk forward. When they reached step six, Jonathan expected to hit the wall, but they didn't until they got to the tenth step and the wall stood before them again. Jonathan knocked on the wall three times and the third door opened. In front of them stood a very regal looking, golden pegasus.

"Yes?" he asked, looking down on them.

Tara stepped forward. "Excuse me, Mr. Pegasus. We're here to find the amulet."

"Really? And who are you?"

"We're the four children from the prophecy." Kelsey chimed in.

"You're a bit small, aren't you?" the pegasus glowered at them.

"And you're quite rude!" Jonathan retorted angrily.

Tara put a calming hand on his shoulder. "Please sir? We've come a long way so far and we have a long way to go."

The pegasus sighed. "Very well, but in future you shall address me as Lieutenant and, between you and I, very soon I shall be Lord Guardian, who is the guy on the inside." He winked at them.

Jonathan shuddered. There was something very creepy about the lieutenant. However, he bit his tongue.

"Can we have the puzzle please?" he asked, through gritted teeth.

"Oh, very well. Here you go. You are standing next to a well and you have two jugs. One jug has a content of 3 litres and the other one has a content of 5 litres. How can you get just 4 litres of water using only these two jugs? You have 10 minutes." He turned the timer over.

This time it was Jonathan's turn to look excited. "I know this!" he shouted, making everyone jump. The lieutenant glared at him.

What is it, Jonathan?" Tara asked in her soft voice.

"I saw it in a film once," he replied as he sat down to think it through.

"Okay. Here we go. You'd have to fill the 5 litre jug. Then fill the 3 litre jug to the top with the water from the 5 litre jug, so that you end up with 2 litres of water in the 5 litre jug. Then you'd dump out the 3 litre jug and pour what's in the 5 litre jug into the 3 litre jug. Then refill the 5 litre jug and fill up the 3 litre jug to the top. Because there was already 2 litres of water in the 3 litre jug, 1 litre goes from the 5 litre jug, leaving 4 litres of water in the 5 litre jug. Is that right?" he turned to look at the lieutenant.

The lieutenant looked quite cross. "I suppose you could say…"

The rest of his sentence was drowned out by the whooping of the children. Jonathan looked quite pleased with himself.

"Very well, you may enter." The lieutenant grumpily opened the door for them, handing them the red key. He stopped Jonathan before he entered. "You want to be very careful young man!" he snarled.

"Is that a threat?" Jonathan challenged, sounding braver than he felt.

"Merely a warning," the lieutenant sneered, letting Jonathan pass.

Once the door was shut, Jonathan ran up to the other children and told them of the lieutenant's warning. Tara gasped. "I didn't like the look of him," she admitted and the others nodded in agreement.

Deciding they'd better find the Lord Guardian and warn him about the lieutenant, they continued on their journey. All around them they could see luscious green trees and beautiful, flowing waterfalls. Jonathan thought this was as close to paradise as they would get and saw the same awe and wonder on the others' faces.

They could hear birds chirping and frogs croaking and even crickets chirruping, but they could see no sign of the Lord Guardian.

"What do we do now?" Kelsey asked, sitting at the stump of a tree.

"Ouch!" a voice came from behind her. Kelsey jumped up with a start. "How would you like it if I sat on your feet?" The tree was talking to them.

The children couldn't help but stare. They had seen many amazing things on their journey so far, but a talking tree was definitely new."

"It's rude to stare," came another voice from behind the tree and out stepped the most dazzling pegasus they had come across. She glistened like diamonds and had the softest, sweetest voice that seemed to tinkle when she laughed.

The children were mesmerised with her beauty until Charlie piped up. "How come you're called Lord Guardian if you're a girl?"

"Shush, Charlie!" Tara hissed, embarrassed.

"That's a fair question," the pegasus answered, looking at Charlie. "It is a tradition that spans across centuries. We do not question it. However, you may all call me Diamanté. Now, I'm assuming that you are the four children who were prophesied."

The children nodded and Diamanté continued. "Do you have all 3 keys?" Again the children nodded.

"Then we must begin." She started humming a hypnotic melody and the children could feel the magic in the air as a chest rose up through the tree and then floated out towards them. The children looked, amazed, at this chest hovering before them.

"Now, only one of you may touch the chest and it must be the one with the purest heart. For if one who is not pure of heart touches the chest, they will be incinerated.

The children looked at each other, scared and moved away to think about it.

"I think it should be Tara, she's the purest," Jonathan said.

"You would say that, you fancy her!" Kelsey grumbled.

Jonathan scowled at his sister, feeling his face grow hot. Tara blushed and looked away.

"Well, how do we decide who's purest?" Jonathan wondered aloud.

Sparks had been listening to the conversation, feeling a bit left out because they'd forgotten him, when he heard someone calling to him. The chest seemed to be glowing brighter and beckoning to him. He knew that if one of the children touched the chest, they may not make it, so he started tugging on Jonathan's jeans.

"Not now Sparks!"

He trotted from one child to the next trying to get some attention, but they all pushed him away, even Kelsey, too consumed with arguing over who would open the chest.

He suddenly jumped up at Jonathan, knocking him over and grabbing the keys, then he set off in a run.

"Come back, Sparks!" Jonathan yelled.

The children looked at Sparks running off. Had he gone mad? Had they made a mistake bringing him along?

Sparks stopped at the chest and the children all ran after him. Jonathan was about to grab the keys back when Tara put a hand on his shoulder. "Just wait a moment," she whispered.

Sparks had the blue key in his mouth and placed it in the first lock. The chest opened and a second chest rose up out of the first. Sparks then picked up the yellow key and placed it in the second lock. Again, the chest opened and a third chest appeared. Finally, he put the red key in the last lock, opened the chest and revealed the amulet. He picked the amulet up in his mouth and bounded over to Jonathan, dropping the amulet in his open hand.

The children looked on in amazement.

Diamanté smiled at them. "You see? Being pure of heart isn't just about being good, it's about being willing to put yourself in danger to protect those that you care about."

Kelsey flung her arms around Sparks. "Good boy!" she cried, making a huge fuss of him. The other children came over and hugged Sparks and Kelsey.

Diamanté smiled at these strange children, wondering if they knew the dangers that lay ahead of them.

"The doorway to the next land is behind that waterfall," she explained, indicating where they needed to go. "Jonathan, I need to speak with you alone."

Jonathan nodded to Tara who took Kelsey and Charlie towards the waterfall.

"What is it?" he asked.

"I need you to be very aware of the dangers you have yet to encounter. Thorn is going to be furious that you have thwarted him so far and will increase his efforts to kill you. It is very likely that you won't succeed or that one, or more, of you won't make it. Are you prepared for this?"

Jonathan gulped and nodded, knowing that he'd protect the others with his last breath.

Diamanté nodded and turned away from him. Jonathan thought she looked sad. "May I give you a warning now?" he asked.

Diamanté looked back at him, surprised. She nodded.

"Be careful of the lieutenant pegasus," he pleaded. "I'm not sure he's on the side of good and I believe he's plotting against you."

Again, Diamanté nodded. "I suspected as much, but thank you for bringing this to my attention. Now you must join your friends."

Jonathan turned to leave, but then flung his arms around Diamanté's neck.

"Thank you," he whispered and walked away, towards the others, not noticing the solitary tear rolling down her face.

CHAPTER 7

THE LAND OF THE TALKING ANIMALS

Jonathan stepped through the waterfall, into a clearing. The suns shone brightly above him. Jonathan had to look twice but, yes, there were two suns.

"The animals are talking," Kelsey whispered.

Jonathan looked at the animals in front of him. Kelsey was right, they were all chatting amongst themselves. He cleared his throat, trying to get their attention, but they ignored him and carried on talking. Tara gave an ear-splitting whistle, stopping everyone in their tracks. Jonathan looked at her in admiration. Was there anything she couldn't do?

He turned to face the animals. "I'm looking for the head animal," he stated, trying to sound commanding and then added "please?" when no one answered him.

A lion stepped forward. "I am Troy. How can I be of assistance?" he asked politely.

Jonathan could have kicked himself. Of course! A lion is the king of beasts, so of course he was going to be the head animal.

"Pleased to meet you," Jonathan said eagerly. "We've come to find the amulet."

Troy looked pleased at this and indicated that the children should follow him.

The other animals watched intently, making the children feel quite uncomfortable, but they supposed they were just as odd to the animals as the animals were to them.

Troy padded ahead of them.

"I'm not sure about this," Tara whispered to Jonathan. "There's something about him I don't trust."

"Like what?" asked Jonathan. "He seems friendly enough, and the lion is traditionally the king of the beasts."

"Yes." Tara agreed. "In our world he is, but we're not in our world."

"I'm sure he's a good lion!" Jonathan persisted, starting to feel cross.

"Well, I'm sure you're right, but I think we should still be on our guard." Tara turned away from him.

Jonathan nodded, feeling guilty that he'd snapped at her.

"Here we are." Troy stopped in front of a cave. "This is my lair. The amulet is inside. Not sure where though, I'm not the most organised of animals," he chuckled.

The children followed Troy into the cave and gazed around. He wasn't kidding when he said he wasn't very organised. There were treasures everywhere. Piles and piles of gold and silver. Jonathan looked puzzled. What would a lion want with all this treasure? He supposed it was to hide the amulet but, oh dear, it was going to take a very long time to find it.

"Right, we'd better start looking." Jonathan rolled his sleeves up.

The children searched through the treasure, but all they could find was gold and silver coins and goblets of all shapes and sizes. Charlie tried to stuff some gold coins into his pockets, but stopped when he saw Tara glaring at him.

"This is hopeless," Tara sighed. "We're never going to find the amulet in all this mess."

"Can't you give us a clue?" Jonathan asked Troy.

"Well…" Troy hesitated. "I'm not really supposed to, but it is for the good of the kingdom. Very well!" he decided. "Have you tried the centre of the cave yet?"

The children looked at each other and then at the centre of the cave. They could see something sparkling on the ground. They looked back at each other in excitement and rushed towards the centre of the cave.

Jonathan bent down to pick it up. "Hang on a moment, this isn't …"

CRASH!

The children jumped as an iron cage crashed down around them.

"Hey, Troy! What's going on? Let us out of here!" Jonathan shouted.

Troy sauntered up to the cage with an evil grin on his face. "Let me think about that for a moment," he said silkily. "No, I don't think I will. Thorn will pay a pretty penny for you four."

The children looked in despair as Troy walked away from them.

"Troy! You can't do this! Let us out!" Jonathan yelled, but the lion had gone to the entrance of the cave, presumably to summon Thorn.

"Jonathan." Tara put a cool hand on his arm. "Save your energy for when you get us out of here."

"What makes you think I'm getting us out of here?" Jonathan replied bitterly.

"Because I have faith in you." She reached up to kiss his cheek.

Jonathan felt a warm glow and smiled back at her.

Kelsey and Charlie rolled their eyes at each other. Teenagers were very annoying. Kelsey looked at the sparkly object on the ground and picked it up. It was just a coin. She sighed. "So, what is Jonathan's amazing plan for getting us out of here?"

Jonathan glared at his sister. "I don't know yet, I'm still..."

He stopped and listened. There was a commotion coming from the entrance of the cave. What was going on?

The children could hear Troy growling and what sounded like an elephant trumpeting and some monkeys chattering. Jonathan hoped these new animals were friendly.

Jonathan?" Kelsey hissed urgently.

"Not now Kels, I'm trying to listen."

But Jonathan, look at ..."

"Kelsey! I'm trying to listen to what's going on."

"JONATHAN!" she screamed.

"What?" he shouted back, looking behind him. But Kelsey wasn't behind him. In fact, no one was in the cage anymore.

"I just thought you'd like to know that Tara's got her special power." Kelsey grinned at him, standing outside the cage.

Jonathan looked at Tara, who shrugged. "I was just holding on to the bar when it came off in my hand," she told him softly.

Jonathan was still looking perplexed when a hoard of monkeys came running through the cave.

"Are you just going to stand there?" one of the monkeys asked impatiently. "Or are you coming with us?"

The children followed the monkeys through the cave to the back. One of the monkeys tapped the boulder, that was sealing them in, three times and the boulder moved.

The children stepped outside and were greeted by bright sunshine and the most enormous elephant they had ever seen.

"What happened!" the elephant boomed.

"Shouldn't we be moving before Troy comes after us?" Jonathan asked, worriedly looking behind them.

"Never mind him. My monkeys will keep him busy. Now, tell me how you came to be trapped by Troy."

"We thought he was the leader, because lions are the king of the animals," Jonathan said guiltily.

"Ha ha ha! Who on earth told you that?" the elephant chuckled.

"It's in all the books." Jonathan was beginning to feel stupid again. This seemed to be happening with increasing frequency.

"That is stuff and nonsense spread about by lions to trick the human world. I am the ruler of all this land. My name is George."

"How do we know you're telling the truth?" Charlie asked rudely.

"Charlie, hush!" Tara admonished.

"The boy has a point. After all, you have already been tricked once!" George replied. "You don't know, not really. But we did just save you from Troy, so I think a little bit of trust can be achieved."

Charlie stuck his tongue out at Tara and nodded at George.

"Now that has been cleared up, please follow me." George turned and walked away.

The children followed him quietly, each wondering what other trials they would have to face on this quest. It had seemed fun at first, but now it just seemed like danger lurked around every corner.

George glanced back at them, guessing what they were thinking, and smiled. They might not believe it, but he knew they were going to succeed and bring peace to all the kingdoms.

He stopped when they reached a big oak tree and tapped with his trunk three times. A doorway opened for them, showing a flight of stairs down into a tunnel.

"Unfortunately I can go no further with you, I am too big." George told them. "I wish you all luck."

Jonathan nodded and led them all down the stairs and through the tunnel. Someone had lit the way for them, so they could see where they had to go. They continued through the tunnel until they reached an underground room. Tara gasped as they entered the brightly lit room. There was a caged lion at the back of the room with the amulet around his neck.

"Cute, isn't he?"

The children whirled round to see Thorn smiling at them. At least, they thought it was a smile. Jonathan shuddered.

"I'll hold him off while you three get the amulet!" Tara shouted.

"Oh that's what you'll do, is it?" Thorn sneered.

Jonathan hesitated.

"Do it, Jonathan!" Tara yelled. "I'll be okay!"

Jonathan nodded and ran to the cage.

"Oh, I will enjoy this." Thorn glided across the floor to her.

"Me too," Tara said grimly, aiming her crossbow.

Jonathan looked back at Tara and felt a rush of pride as he watched Tara do battle with Thorn. She may not be as fast as him, but she was definitely as strong, if not stronger.

"Jon!" Kelsey shouted urgently. "Come on! We've got to get the amulet!"

The caged lion growled at them and tried to scratch them through the cage. Suddenly he was thrown back. The children looked at the lion, alarmed. Kelsey went to touch the cage.

"Don't Kels!" Jonathan shrieked. "I think the cage is electrified."

The lion got gingerly to his feet and started licking his paw. Kelsey looked desperately at him. "What do we do now?"

Jonathan thought for a moment. "Let me get my sword, I'll try and pick the lock."

Kelsey gave him the knife. "Please be careful, Jon. If you touch the cage you'll get hurt."

Jonathan nodded and started working on the lock, praying that it wasn't electrified too. Luckily, it wasn't. He concentrated on the lock and kept working on it until he heard a click. The cage door had opened.

He heard a scream. Tara! He turned around to see Thorn looming over him and Tara lying on the ground.

"Thank you for getting me my amulet." Thorn grinned.

"It's not yours! It's ours!" Jonathan stood his ground, sounding braver than he felt.

"Careful boy!" Thorn snarled. "I haven't bitten your girlfriend yet, but I will do if you don't hand the amulet over."

Jonathan looked over at Tara, stricken.

"No Jon, you can't." Kelsey was crying.

"I'm sorry Kels, I can't let her die." Jonathan turned to crouch next to the lion, who seemed more amenable now he was out of the cage.

"I'm sorry," he whispered as he slid the amulet over the lions head.

He stood up just as he heard a thump. He spun around and saw Tara grinning at him, with a huge boulder in her hands and Thorn lying spark-out on the floor. Sparks was trotting up and down Thorn, occasionally puffing little flames at him.

Jonathan laughed. "Okay, let's go then."

"How do we get out of here?" Tara asked, puzzled.

Jonathan looked around him, but couldn't see an exit anywhere. He felt a tug on his trousers and looked down. The little lion was trying to pull him towards the cage. Jonathan looked inside and saw a bright, shimmering light.

"I think we have to go through that light," he said.

Tara looked at him doubtfully, but said nothing as he pushed Kelsey and Charlie through and they disappeared. Next, Sparks and the little lion bounded through. Tara knelt down and looked at the light.

"Oh well, here goes," she said, closing her eyes.

Jonathan took one last look at the room, and at Thorn, then crawled into the light himself.

CHAPTER 8

GNOME DOME

"Aaargh!" the children screamed as they were spinning through the portal.

Jonathan thought they'd never stop spinning when… "Oof!" They'd landed on something soft.

"Get off me! Get off me!" came some voices underneath them.

The children stood up and looked down. Glaring up at them were the queerest little men they had ever seen.

"Oh, what lovely little men." Tara gushed.

Jonathan thought they looked quite ugly, but wisely said nothing.

"Who are you calling lovely, lady?" one of the little men shouted.

"Jon," said Kelsey. "They look just like the little men in our garden."

Jonathan slapped his head. "Of course! You're gnomes!" he addressed the little men.

"We know what **we** are! What are you?" grumbled one of the gnomes.

"Well, we're the children sent to save you."

"Does it look like we need saving?" another gnome piped up. "The only thing we need saving from is idiot children that fall out of the sky and try squashing us!"

"That was an accident. We didn't mean to." Jonathan was starting to get cross with these little gnomes.

"Yes, a likely story. You just wanted to take our gold! Greedy! And thieves as well!"

The gnomes glared at the children and walked away, still grumbling.

"What unpleasant little gnomes," Tara said quietly. "I hope not everyone here is that grumpy."

"Let's have a look around and try and get our bearings," Jonathan suggested.

The others agreed and they started looking around their new surroundings. They were so engrossed in watching the hustle and bustle of the gnome village that they didn't hear the whir of the portal opening again, or the soft thud as a pair of feet landed on the grass and they didn't hear the evil chuckle as a pair of gleaming eyes watched them.

"I think we should split up," Tara said. "We'll cover more ground that way."

"I dunno," Jonathan replied, doubtfully, looking at Kelsey and Charlie.

"Kelsey and Charlie can take Sparks and the little lion with them, for protection."

"My name's Tony." the little lion spoke.

The children looked at him, amazed. "We didn't know you could speak," Tara admitted.

"Of course I can speak. I come from The Land of the Talking Animals." Tony huffed.

"Sorry Tony, I never thought." Tara apologised. "Would you mind protecting Kelsey and Charlie?" Sparks growled at her. "With Sparks' help, of course."

"Yes, of course." Tony nodded. "Come on children, we'll go this way. I'm sure there are some sweet shops over there."

At the mention of sweet shops Kelsey and Charlie hurried excitedly after Tony, with Sparks trotting playfully beside them.

Jonathan looked at Tara self-consciously. "Well, I'll go that way," he mumbled, pointing towards the woods.

Tara nodded, sighing slightly as she watched his retreating back. Jonathan was definitely cute, but it looked as though she'd die of old age before he asked her out.

Jonathan made his way through the woods, using the sword to hack the branches.

"That's not a very nice thing to do. Trees do have feelings you know."

Jonathan turned around slowly, willing himself to not see the person it was.

Thorn stood there, idly watching him.

"Someone needs to get you a bell," Jonathan grumbled.

"I shall remember to put it on my Christmas list. Now, you really need to hand me the amulets."

"Yeah? And why would I do that?" Jonathan scoffed.

"Because I have your father." Thorn's voice had become very low and soft and Jonathan was having a hard time concentrating. What was that about his father?

"The amulets are mine and I need you to get more for me, to keep your father safe."

"Safe," Jonathan repeated in a monotone.

"Now, give me the amulets, like a good boy."

Jonathan handed the satchel over to Thorn and Thorn swapped it with a satchel of his own.

"This is your new satchel of amulets and you must collect the other amulets for me."

"Yes Master." Jonathan nodded, the hypnosis complete.

"Good boy. Now go off to meet your friends, but remember, do not tell them what has happened here."

Thorn laughed softly to himself as he watched Jonathan stumble to the edge of the woods. Foolish boy! Foolish human boy! Humans were so susceptible, it was child's play. Looking down at his new amulets, he felt a grim sense of satisfaction. Things were finally going his way.

Jonathan reached the town centre, still feeling a bit dazed.

"Are you okay, Jonathan?" Tara asked, worried.

Jonathan shook himself awake. "I'm fine!" He waved her away. "Anyone have any luck?"

They all shook their heads.

"What ya looking for?" a cheeky voice behind them asked.

The children looked around to see five of the most colourful gnomes they had met so far. They were all the colours of the rainbow.

The gnomes grinned at them. "Let's introduce ourselves," one of them said. "I'm Sloan, this is Tone, Roam, Joan and Jerome. We're The Friendlies."

"Wow, you like your rhyming names, don't you?" Jonathan scoffed.

"Jonathan!" Tara was shocked. This wasn't like Jonathan at all.

"Yes, we do." Sloan said, not noticing anything strange. "Come and play with us. We haven't had anyone to play with us in such a long time and the other gnomes are so grumpy."

Tara thought about the other gnomes and nodded in agreement. "Don't other people visit, that you can play with?"

"No. People are scared of the curse."

"What curse?" Jonathan asked, in spite of himself.

The gnomes indicated that the children should sit.

"Some gnomes had gone travelling to Witch Town when they came across an empty cottage. Inside there were piles of gold. Now, most gnomes aren't greedy and selfish, just grumpy, but these gnomes wanted some of that gold for themselves. So they each filled a satchel full of the gold and hurried back to our village. Shortly afterwards, a fearsome witch came and said that if the gnomes, that had stolen her gold, came forward and returned it, then she'd say no more about it. But the gnomes were too afraid to come forward and the witch grew angry. The angrier she became, the more she seemed to grow until she must have been 10 feet at least. She said in a booming voice that, because of the deceit and treachery of those few gnomes, she was putting a curse on the entire land. A huge dome crashed down around us all and no gnome can leave the dome. There is supposed to be a door in the wall of the dome, but it's invisible and moves a lot, so no gnome has ever found it."

"Wow! That was quite a story!" Tara remarked.

The Friendlies looked pleased about entertaining them. "Now, you play with us?" they asked hopefully.

"I'm sorry, we can't," explained Tara. "We have to find the amulet."

The Friendlies jumped up and down excitedly. "We know where it is!" the Friendly called Jerome told them. "It's over there, in the head gnome's house."

The children looked at where Jerome was pointing. It was a beautiful yellow cottage with honeysuckle entwining the arbour at the side of the front porch.

"Great, let's go!" Jonathan said impatiently.

Tara glared at him. He was being very rude all of a sudden.

"Thank you for all your help," she said to The Friendlies. "Perhaps Sparks and Tony would like to play with you whilst we get the amulet."

"Yes, we can do that." Tony replied happily.

"Excellent," said Sloan. "Be careful though, because the head gnome is the grumpiest of them all."

Tara nodded and she and the others walked up to the cottage, taking in the beautiful fragrance of the honeysuckle.

Jonathan knocked on the door and waited for the gnome to answer. The door opened a crack. "What do you want?" a voice said rudely through the crack.

"I'm Tara. This is Jonathan…" Tara started.

"I didn't ask who you were! I asked what you wanted!" the gnome interrupted.

"We want the amulet." Jonathan replied, just as rudely.

Tara shook her head. "Please sir. We've come for the amulet. It's very important."

"Not to me, it isn't and you're not having it, so nah!" The gnome stuck his tongue out at them and slammed the door shut.

"Well, he was rude!" Jonathan said, grumpily.

"You weren't much better yourself." Tara was on the verge of tears. "What's the matter with you, Jonathan?"

"Nothing's the matter with me. I just want to get the amulets as quickly as possible for my mas - the fairies, so we can get home."

Tara said nothing, but looked at him strangely.

"So, how are we going to get the amulet?" Kelsey asked.

"We need to lure him out somehow, Jonathan replied, avoiding Tara's watchful gaze. "I know! Kelsey, you and Charlie throw stones at the back of the cottage and, when he comes out to investigate, Tara and I will go in and look for the amulet." He grinned, feeling quite pleased with himself.

"Isn't that rather dangerous? What if he catches Kelsey and Charlie?" Tara asked.

"He won't! And, if he does, well, then they should have been faster, shouldn't they?" he answered, impatiently.

Tara stared at him, astounded that he could be so callous. She was about to tell him so when he interrupted again.

"Well, are we going or not?"

Kelsey glared at him. "Yes, your Majesty!" she said sarcastically and ran around to he back.

Tara and Jonathan hid behind some trees and soon saw the head gnome come out of his cottage and start shouting at Kelsey and Charlie.

"Come on!" Jonathan urged as they ran towards the cottage. "I'll check downstairs, you check upstairs."

Tara nodded curtly and ran up the stairs. Jonathan went into the living room and started looking under cushions, throwing them on the floor. He looked under the table and some chairs, but still no amulet. He was about to go into the kitchen when he heard Tara shriek upstairs. What now? Honestly, that girl was hard work. Once he'd given his master the amulets, perhaps he could be turned, like his father, so he wouldn't have to deal with silly girls anymore. He ran up the stairs to find Tara.

"What is it?" he asked when he found her.

"I thought I saw a mouse," she replied. "It's gone now, but I did find this." She held up the amulet to show him.

Jonathan snatched the amulet off her, with a gleam in his eye and took a good look at it.

"Great, let's go!" He spun on his heel and walked out of the room, with the amulet in his hand. Tara looked after him with tears in her eyes. She didn't know what had happened to him, but this was not the Jonathan she knew. Or perhaps it was, and the kind, caring Jonathan had just been an act.

She ran after him and they stepped out of the front door, just as Kelsey and Charlie ran around to the front of the house, with the gnome in hot pursuit.

The gnome looked at Jonathan then at the amulet. "THIEF!" he shrieked.

"Run!" Jonathan shouted and the children ran as fast as they could, with the gnome closely behind.

They ran through the woods, weaving in and out of the trees, but still the gnome was chasing them. They reached the edge of the woods and kept running, not daring to look behind them. Now there were no houses, no trees, nothing to hide behind. They heard a growl behind them. Tony and Sparks had joined the chase and they were snapping at the gnome's heels.

"Ow! Gerroff!" the gnome shouted at them, trying to kick them out of the way. But Sparks and Tony were too fast and sped out to join the children.

Jonathan was beginning to think they were going to be running forever when…

"Oof!" Charlie bounced back. They had reached the edge of the dome.

"Now what do we do?" Tara looked back to see the gnome gaining on them. "The door could be anywhere."

"We'll never find it!" Kelsey complained, leaning on the dome wall. "Aaargh!" Jonathan looked at the wall. Kelsey had disappeared.

"Look!" Tara pointed. "Kelsey went through the wall."

Kelsey was standing there waving at them from outside the dome. The children looked back and saw the gnome, almost upon them, then they looked at the dome wall and ran straight for the spot Kelsey had disappeared through, praying it hadn't moved.

Jonathan shut his eyes as he reached the wall and walked through a jellylike substance to reach the other side. He looked back to see the gnome banging on the dome wall and screaming at them. He laughed and held up the amulet, kissing it.

Elsewhere, Thorn was watching the scene unfold with an evil grin. Soon he would have all the amulets and perhaps the children could join their father. He let out a deep chuckle as he looked over to the pathetic man, cowering in the corner.

CHAPTER 9

TROLL TERRITORY

The children ran as fast as they could, away from the dome; into a dark, dank forest.

"Ouch!" shouted Charlie, rubbing his shoulder. Something sharp had just hit him. The children looked around them and saw ugly little men, throwing spears at them.

"What are they?" Tara yelled, fearfully.

"Who cares?" Jonathan replied. "Run!"

The children ran through the forest, fending off spears and boulders, that the little men seemed to pick up effortlessly.

"Why aren't they coming any closer?" Kelsey cried.

Again, Jonathan shouted, "Who cares?"

Kelsey glared at him. Tara shook her head. "I think they're too scared to come any closer." she reassured Kelsey.

"I think they're trolls!" Charlie yelled over the din. "I've seen pictures of them in my colouring books."

"Great!" Jonathan said sarcastically. "Now we know what they are, how do we get rid of them?"

The children thought for a moment.

"I know!" Tara exclaimed, as she ducked from another flying boulder. "Charlie can use his vision to spot the trolls, in their hiding places, and I can throw boulders back at them."

Kelsey and Charlie nodded enthusiastically.

"Fine!" Jonathan said grumpily. "Let's go!"

"Fine!" Tara retorted angrily and stalked off.

"Tara! Over there!" Charlie shouted, pointing to his right.

Tara picked up a boulder and threw it in the direction Charlie pointed. They heard a thud and a scream and knew she'd hit her target.

Every time Charlie spotted a troll, Tara threw a boulder at them. Sometimes she hit them, sometimes she had to duck from the boulders flying towards her.

Finally they reached the edge of the forest and looked back at the nasty, ugly little creatures, who were hopping up and down and shouting angrily.

Looking ahead of them, they saw a cave.

"Not another cave!" Kelsey grumbled.

"Shut up Kels!" Jonathan snapped.

"Jonathan!" Tara was shocked that he could speak to his sister like that.

"Have you lot quite finished?" a grumpy voice came from the mouth of the cave.

The children turned and two guards stood before them, either side of the largest black dragon they had ever seen.

"Alright, alright." Another troll came out of the cave. He glanced at Jonathan, knowingly. "I suppose you are all here for the amulet," he sneered. "I'm Trickster, the head troll."

"Yes." Tara nodded.

"Very well! You will have many dangers to face in this cave, to reach the amulet. First you must fight the guards. They may not look frightening, but they have been trained to fight to the death."

The children looked at each other, afraid.

"Then you must get past our dragon. She is fiercely protective, will breathe fire and the spikes in her tail have been dipped in poison."

"If you are still alive after this, you must defeat the dangers in the cave itself. I cannot tell you what these will be, but you must be on your guard."

Kelsey, Charlie and Tara clung to each other in trepidation. Jonathan stood to one side, looking bored.

Trickster continued. "If you have survived all these trials, there are three enchantments, surrounding the amulet, that you must break. If you succeed in breaking these enchantments, you may take the amulet. If you fail, you will be trapped and stay here, with me, forever. Do you understand?"

The children nodded bleakly.

"Then let the games begin!" Trickster smirked.

The two guard trolls stood with their spears out in front of them, looking menacingly. The dragon snorted, puffing flames at the children.

"Hey, watch it!" Jonathan yelled, as one flame came uncomfortably close to him. He motioned for the others to gather around him.

"Okay. We've got to get past the guards and the dragon," he said importantly.

"Well duh!" Charlie retorted rudely.

Jonathan glared at him. "Tara and I will fight the guard trolls and Sparks can cuddle up to the dragon and distract her. Then Kelsey and Charlie can sneak into the cave and we'll join them when we've defeated the guards."

Tara nodded. It was a solid plan and she was relieved Jonathan was acting more like himself.

"Okay, let's do this," she said as the guards rushed for them.

Tara yelped as a spear went into her leg. Picking the spear up, with the troll on the end of it, she flung it to the far corner of the cave where it slumped to the ground. She glanced over at Jonathan, who was now doing hand-to-hand combat with his troll, the spear nowhere to be found.

Sparks, she found, was whimpering and getting the dragon's attention. The dragon opened up her wings and welcomed Sparks, who lay down next to the dragon.

Kelsey and Charlie had run ahead and were now looking back at the fighting going on behind them. They heard a scream and a whoosh as Jonathan's troll flew over their heads.

"Let's go!" Jonathan ordered.

"Wait!" Tara shouted.

"What now?" came Jonathan's impatient reply.

"Just listen!"

The children listened and they could hear a rumbling sound.

"What the ..."

A boulder swung in front of them. Then another. Kelsey screamed as one just missed the top of her head.

"Run!" Jonathan pushed them all ahead, stopping short before another boulder swung past them. They ran towards a barrier and leaped over it, into another chamber of the cave. Before they could catch their breath, the ground started trembling.

"What's going on?" Kelsey whimpered.

"I don't know!" Tara looked fearfully back at her.

The ground started cracking and vines swept up through the ground, twisting and squirming, snapping at their ankles.

Jonathan got his sword out and started hacking at the vines. Tara screamed as a vine crept around her ankle, dragging her to the ground. Jonathan leaped over to her and chopped the vine in half. Tara looked up at him, gratefully, but he stared blankly back at her. Jonathan, making way for Tara, continued to swing his sword through the vines, whilst Charlie and Kelsey crawled through.

All of a sudden, the ground stopped shaking and everything was still. Eerily so. A shimmering green light was shining ahead of them. Hypnotised, they moved towards it and stepped into the Chamber of Enchantments. They gazed around in wonder.

"We made it," Tara whispered.

"Not quite." Jonathan replied gruffly, as he looked around the chamber himself. He knew Thorn had helped him get this far and was wondering how he was going to get the amulet for his master, when he heard Thorn's voice.

"Move to the first enchantment, read the inscription. Then cover your ears or you will not leave this place," came the silky warning.

Jonathan walked towards the enchantment and read the inscription:

Our voices are beautiful, but not to be heard.
If you listen, strange things will occur.

Jonathan looked at the others, who looked puzzled.

"Well? Isn't it obvious?" he said. "We have to put our hands over our ears, so we don't hear their voices!"

Tara looked at him strangely, but agreed with him.

Putting their hands over their ears, they could hear muffled sounds, but no voices. When they could no longer hear anything, they removed their hands and breathed a collective sigh of relief. Jonathan started to make his way to the second enchantment when he heard a yelp. He looked at Tara, who was looking back, horrified. Charlie was standing in the same spot, frozen.

"He must have listened." Tara wept.

"Well there's nothing we can do for him! Stupid boy!" Jonathan shouted angrily.

"That stupid boy is my brother and I'm not leaving him!" Tara retorted, just as angrily.

"Be careful," the voice in Jonathan's head said.

Jonathan sighed. "I'm sorry. There is nothing we can do for him. Maybe when we get to Witch Town, a spell will set him free."

Kelsey slipped her hand into Tara's and Tara calmed down. "You're right," she breathed. "I know you're right. I just can't bear to see him like this."

Jonathan nodded, as Sparks came bounding up to them.

"I know!" Kelsey said. "Sparks can look after Charlie, until we get him back. Can't you, Sparks?" Sparks nodded and stood solemnly next to Charlie.

"Okay then. Let's go!" Jonathan walked to the next enchantment. Tara glared at his back.

Jonathan stopped in front of a pedestal, the amulet wrapped around a golden statue. He went to touch it. *"STOP!"* the voice commanded in his head. He pulled his hand back, just as some thorns shot up, almost piercing his skin.

"That was lucky!" Tara looked at him.

"Yes, it was," he murmured.

He removed his sword and placed it underneath the amulet. Thorns rose, but broke when they met with the cold steel. He lifted the amulet gently from its home and glided the sword slowly towards himself. Grabbing the amulet off the sword and pocketing it, he hurried to the final enchantment with Tara and Kelsey following him.

"This enchantment is tricky," Thorn's voice echoed. *"It will show you what you want to see. If you believe it, you will be trapped."*

The children stepped forward and read the inscription:

The place you want to be...

"Oh," Kelsey gasped. "So pretty!"

"What is it?" Jonathan asked sharply.

"I'm in Fairyland and all the fairies are playing. They want me to play with them."

"What are you talking about?" Tara asked. "We're back at school. I can see all my friends."

Jonathan was about to tell them it was an illusion, when he saw his father come up to him and give him a hug. But his father was a vampire. How could this be? He tried pulling away from his father's grasp, but his grip tightened.

"No!" he shouted, closing his eyes. "Get off me! You're not real!"

He opened his eyes and his father was gone.

He turned to Kelsey and Tara. "Snap out of it! It's not real! They're illusions to keep you here. Shut your eyes!" he yelled.

Tara looked at him oddly and Kelsey pouted. "I wanna play with the fairies."

"Well you can't!" Jonathan put his hand over her eyes.

"Hey!" Kelsey pushed him away. "Where did they go?"

"They were never there. It wasn't real." Jonathan sighed.

Tara continued looking at him. "Why aren't you in your uniform, Jonathan? You'll get into trouble."

Kelsey looked at Jonathan in despair.

"Sorry," Jonathan replied apologetically, before tackling her to the ground.

"What are you doing? Are you mad?" she screamed.

Jonathan got up, helping Tara up with him. "You're welcome!" he glared at her.

"It was a 'lusion," Kelsey explained.

"An illusion," Jonathan corrected.

"Wow! That was powerful!" Tara gasped.

A creak made them look up and a door appeared before them.

"Shall we?" Jonathan asked, opening the door to the next land.

CHAPTER 10

GOBLIN GLEN

The children followed Jonathan through the door into a clearing.

Where are we now? Jonathan thought. *You are in Goblin Glen,* came the voice inside him. *You must be careful. The goblins will try and trick you.*

Jonathan nodded inwardly and said to the rest of the group, "Shall we look around?"

Tara and Kelsey agreed, but both were rather subdued, having left Charlie and Sparks behind.

Kelsey gasped. Up ahead was an eerie, glowing green light.

Jonathan saw it too. "We'd better be careful," he said. "We don't have much luck with glowing lights."

"Good point," replied Tara, glad that Jonathan appeared to be his old self again.

They crept towards the green glow until they came to the entrance of a mine. They carefully stepped over the threshold and held their breath. Nothing!

"OW!" shouted Kelsey as she fell over.

"What happened?" Jonathan asked impatiently. "You really want to be more careful Kels."

Kelsey glared at him. "It wasn't my fault! I got tripped over by something."

"By what? There's nothing here." Jonathan scoffed.

"Wait!" Tara exclaimed. "I can hear something."

They listened and could hear giggling.

"What on earth…" Jonathan began.

A whoosh came by him and he landed, rather inelegantly, on his backside as a blur ran past him.

"Hey! Stop that!" he yelled at the blur.

The blur stopped and grinned at the children.

"Shan't!" he said rudely, sticking his tongue out at them.

"Please!" Tara begged quietly. "We're tired and we're hungry. Please just let us sit and eat for a while."

The blur and his friends huddled together.

"Alright," he said, after much deliberation. I'm Growly the Goblin. You can sit and eat, but then we continue."

Continue what? Jonathan wondered as they opened their backpack to get food.

They looked inside… it was empty! Where was all the food?

"We must have eaten it all," whined Kelsey.

"I don't think so!" grumbled Jonathan, looking suspiciously at the goblins.

Marching up to them, he demanded, "Where's our food?"

Growly looked back innocently. "What food?"

"The food you stole from us!"

Tara put a hand on his shoulder. "Calm down Jonathan, you have no proof."

"No proof! NO PROOF! Where did it go then, Miss Know It All?" Jonathan exploded.

"JONATHAN!" Kelsey exclaimed as Tara tried not to cry.

The goblins watched this exchange with great interest, guessing that Jonathan was under Thorn's spell.

Smiling slyly, Growly said, "If you want food, I can give you food… for a price."

"What kind of price?" Tara asked suspiciously.

"That ring on your finger. Is it real gold?"

"Yes." Tara replied. "It is."

"The ring for some food then!" the goblin told her.

Tara sighed and looked at the ring. It had been a present off her mother. But they needed food. Sadly, she slid the ring off her finger and handed it over to the goblins. Growly grabbed the ring and threw a loaf of stale bread at them. "Here you go!" he cackled.

"Great!" said Jonathan. "Just fantastic!"

"Well, I didn't see you coming up with any bright ideas!" retorted Tara, close to tears.

"Let's just eat," Kelsey said gloomily.

They plodded their way through the stale bread, feeling more and more queasy. When they felt they couldn't eat anymore, they stood up.

"Where are the goblins?" Kelsey asked.

They looked around everywhere, but they couldn't see them.

"Maybe they decided they were no match for us," Jonathan chuckled.

"Or maybe they're getting ready to trick us!" Tara glared at Jonathan.

"Let's go through there, I can hear voices." Kelsey pointed to a doorway.

The children stepped through the doorway, where they met the goblins again.

"I see you've found our secret chamber," Growly sneered.

Jonathan couldn't see what was so secret about this room, but wisely said nothing.

"I expect you're after the amulet."

The children nodded.

"Very well! Here are three tunnels. You have to pick the correct one. One will lead to the amulet. One will lead to your deaths. And one will lead to you being captured and staying here for eternity."

The children looked at each other in fear and then looked at the tunnels. They each glowed a different colour: red, green and blue. Which one should they choose?

Jonathan heard some hissing as Thorn was thinking. *The amulet is red, so logically the tunnel must be red also.*

'Don't you know?' Jonathan asked Thorn.

The goblins offer allegiance to no one, not even me, Thorn hissed.

Jonathan sighed. "We've got to pick one," he said to the girls.

"Really Einstein! I had no idea!" Tara said sarcastically.

Jonathan glared at her. "What I meant was we might just as well choose one and get it over with. There's no way to work it out logically."

Tara sighed. Jonathan was right, even if he was acting a bit weird.

"Okay then, which one shall we choose?"

Jonathan appeared to be pondering the dilemma. "How about the red one? It's as good a choice as any."

Tara and Kelsey nodded and followed Jonathan down the red tunnel. The goblins were giggling and whispering either side of them. Jonathan glared at them, which made them laugh even more.

The children ran down the tunnel, towards the red glow, trying to put as much distance between them and the creepy goblins as they could.

They reached the end of the tunnel and started searching for the amulet. Where was it? It wasn't here! Tara looked at Jonathan in dismay.

CLANG!

They whirled around to see a huge iron gate drop down. Oh no! The goblins caught up to them.

"I hope you enjoy your eternal stay with us!" Growly chortled.

"When I get out of here, I'll..." Jonathan started.

"You're going nowhere!" Growly said menacingly. "And there's nothing you or your master can do about it!"

Jonathan could hear Thorn roaring in his head. He wouldn't be happy with Jonathan when they got out of there... if they got out of there. Tara tried bending the bars, but they wouldn't budge. The goblins must have used some sort of magic.

The children looked at the metal bars and the goblins. What were they going to do now?

CHAPTER 11

BROWNIE'S BOROUGH

The children stared at each other, gloomily, whilst the goblins giggled with glee. A crash sounded in the distance and made Growly and his friends jump up with a start. They rushed to the tunnel entrance.

"Ow!"

"Oof!"

"Gerroff!"

The children looked in interest to see what was going on, but all they could see was a dim light.

The light was coming towards them and getting brighter. The children clung onto each other in trepidation. They looked up and saw five little men with silvery beards following the light.

"Hello children," said one of the little men. "I'm Bobby the Brownie and we've come to rescue you."

The children looked at the brownies sceptically.

"How do we know you're friendly?" Jonathan asked sharply.

"You don't, but you don't really have much choice, do you?" Bobby replied wisely.

The brownies held hands and muttered a few words. Within moments, the iron bars had disappeared and the children were free.

"Now, follow me!" Bobby ordered as he led the children down the tunnel. "Down here." He pointed down another tunnel with a green glow.

They all rushed down the tunnel and saw the amulet stuck to a large rock at the end. Jonathan tugged on the amulet, but it wouldn't budge. The children all pulled and pulled, but to no avail.

"Use your sword!" Bobby said urgently. Jonathan got his sword out and started swinging at the stone.

Clang! Clang! went the sword.

The goblins, hearing this commotion, came rushing to the tunnel. Just as the children freed the amulet and the goblins entered the tunnel, the brownies muttered another spell and they were all transported to another tunnel.

"Woah, head rush!" Jonathan said, sitting down.

"You have no time to sit. We must move!" Bobby ushered them all through the tunnel until they reached daylight. When their eyes adjusted to the light, they looked around. They were surrounded by the most beautiful, quaint little cottages.

"Wow! So pretty!" Kelsey gasped.

"We must hurry. The next amulet is in my house," Bobby said. "Please, all come with me and you can have a good meal and a restful night's sleep."

"I thought we were in a hurry." Jonathan said sharply.

Tara glared at him.

"We are, but you'll be no use to anyone if you're tired and hungry and you still have a great many dangers to face."

The children followed Bobby and entered his cottage.

"Betty, we're home!" Bobby called out to his wife.

A face peered around the doorway.

"Oh, hello children. Please come and sit down. Dinner will be ready in a few minutes."

The children sat down and smelled the wonderful aroma coming from the kitchen. Betty brought in plates of fish and chips. The children dug in, as though they hadn't eaten for months, which it felt like they hadn't. For dessert, Betty brought in the most decadent looking pavlova the children had ever seen.

After their bellies were full and their eyes started drifting, Betty showed them to their rooms.

Kelsey and Tara fell asleep almost immediately. Jonathan lay on his bed, thinking hard.

"Jonathan, you need to come to me," Thorn hissed in his head.

"Where?" Jonathan asked.

"To the forest."

Kelsey awoke with a start. What was that she just heard? She listened again. She could hear someone asking Jonathan to meet them. Puzzled, she went downstairs to tell Bobby. Bobby listened carefully as she told him.

"It sounds like Jonathan is under Thorn's spell. Has he been acting differently lately?"

Kelsey thought back to all the times Jonathan had shouted at them and been nasty recently. "Yes!" she exclaimed.

"I have a spell to break the hypnosis, but we must act quickly."

They heard a noise in the hallway and Kelsey rushed in holding a frying pan.

CRASH!

Jonathan slumped to the floor.

Bobby and Kelsey dragged Jonathan into the kitchen. This took a while, because neither Bobby nor Kelsey were very big and Jonathan was a teenage boy.

Sitting him in a chair, they tied him up. Bobby produced a potion from one of his kitchen cupboards and muttered a few words. "Once he has drunk this, he will no longer be under Thorn's spell."

Holding Jonathan's head back, they poured the potion down his throat. Jonathan instantly started coughing and spluttering. When he had stopped, he looked around and saw Kelsey and Bobby. He looked at them in horror as the realisation of what he had done dawned on him. Looking down at the rope tied around him, he said, "Kels, let me out please?"

Bobby looked at Jonathan sternly. "Kelsey, listen to Jonathan's thoughts and tell me what you hear?"

Kelsey concentrated for a moment. "Just a bunch of stuff about Tara." Jonathan blushed.

Bobby quickly untied him and Jonathan explained what had happened. "Thorn's got all the amulets!" he groaned.

Bobby instructed Kelsey to wake Tara up. They were going on a trip to the forest.

15 minutes later; Tara, Kelsey and Bobby were hiding and Jonathan went to meet Thorn.

"Do you have any more amulets for me?" Thorn sneered.

"Yes." Jonathan replied, nervously.

Behind the bushes, Kelsey was working hard to block Thorn from reading Jonathan's mind. A small, dishevelled man was standing nearby, holding the bag of amulets.

Tara whispered something to Kelsey and went deeper into the forest, whistling as she went.

Jonathan's father glanced up as she moved past him and followed her. Once they were out of sight and earshot, Tara picked up a branch and hit Jonathan's father over the head. She grabbed the bag and replaced it with the replicas that Bobby had made. Rushing back to the bushes, she was just in time to see Jonathan give Thorn the fake amulets.

"Good!" Thorn said. "I'll be in touch. You may go!" Thorn glided away into the forest.

Breathing a sigh of relief, the children and Bobby made their way back to the cottage. "It won't fool Thorn for long, but it will buy you some time," Bobby told them as he led them down to the basement.

In the basement there was an enormous box, with hundreds of locks.

"Is the amulet in there?" Jonathan asked.

Bobby nodded and, with a flick of his wrist, opened all the locks.

"You may have this amulet on one condition. That I get to keep Tony. We're in need of a new lion." The children looked puzzled, but agreed.

Bobby tapped on the box three times and it moved aside. Saying one final goodbye to Bobby, and Tony, the children walked through the opening to the next land.

CHAPTER 12

THE LAND OF THE LEPRECHAUNS

Jonathan, Tara and Kelsey stepped through the opening and almost stumbled down the vast stairs in front of them.

"Who puts stairs at the entrance of a new land?" Jonathan grumbled.

Tara glanced nervously at him, worried that he might still be under Thorn's spell, but Kelsey giggled.

"Glad to have you back to normal, Jon," and she started skipping down the stairs.

"Shall we?" Tara asked timidly, but Jonathan put a hand out to stop her.

"I'm so sorry for everything I said and did whilst I was under Thorn's control," he apologised, tears in his eyes.

Tara placed her hand on his. "It's okay, Jonathan. You couldn't help it. I'm just glad you're back to normal." She smiled at him.

Jonathan smiled back and held out his hand for her. She took it, grinning, and they walked down the long staircase together. When they reached the bottom, they saw Kelsey chatting to a portly looking gentleman.

"Hey you two, what took you so long?" Kelsey called out to them cheerfully. "This is Larry, the head leprechaun."

"It's a pleasure to meet ye," Larry said in a pleasant Irish brogue.

Jonathan went to shake Larry's hand, "pleased to meet you, sir."

"Now, we'll have none of that. Just call me Larry," Larry insisted.

"Okay, Larry." Jonathan replied.

"I heard ye were coming, let me show ye round."

The children followed Larry to the town square and they looked on in wonder at all the hustle and bustle.

"Oh look!" gasped Tara, pointing at the most adorable little dress shop she had ever seen. It was the colour of emeralds and the dresses sparkled like diamonds.

Jonathan followed her gaze and immediately saw a creature who was most decidedly not a leprechaun.

"Who's that, Larry?" Jonathan asked nervously.

"That is a problem." Larry replied. "Quick, in here."

He ushered the children into a small ornate room, where six other leprechauns were sitting, looking at them expectantly.

"Jonathan, Tara and Kelsey, meet the Council of Leprechauns. Linda, Luke, Lucy, Lottie, Leopold and Leila," Larry rattled off.

"Pleased to meet you," the children shook each of the leprechauns' hands.

"Now, the Council of Leprechauns shall come to order!" Larry boomed, very importantly.

Linda waved a hand at him. "Never mind all the formalities. We have a vampire problem and we need to get rid of them. So, what do we do to minimise casualties?"

"Evacuate!" Lucy called out. "We can't fight vampires!" Leopald and Leila nodded along to her. "Hear hear!" they cried out.

"We can't leave our homes though!" Luke glared at her.

"Absolutely right!" Lottie added. "We need to fight for our homes."

Luke nodded continuing, "We might not be as strong as them, but we must have a few tricks up our sleeves."

"That's it!" Kelsey exclaimed, making everyone jump.

"What's it, little girl?" Lucy asked impatiently. "We are not waiting around to be vampire fodder."

Kelsey ignored her and continued. "What if we played tricks on the vampires?"

"What kind of tricks, Kels?" Jonathan asked curiously.

Kelsey thought for a moment and then explained her plan. Jonathan, Tara and Larry looked at her in amazement. It was a solid plan. The other leprechauns took a bit more convincing, but soon came on board. Jonathan ruffled Kelsey's hair and Kelsey beamed proudly.

"Right, let's get started then," Larry said, rubbing his hands together. He was starting the plan off, whilst everyone else worked behind the scenes.

The children watched as Larry walked up to the podium in the town square.

"Ladies and gentlemen," he started, "We have an impromptu performance for our esteemed guests," he nodded at the vampires.

"Come here in an hour for the show of a lifetime!"

The vampires sneered at Larry, but looked interested nonetheless.

Larry bowed with a flourish and rushed off.

"Right!" said Jonathan. "We have an hour to set everything up."

"And what if we can't?" Lucy asked fearfully.

"We will!" Jonathan said with more confidence than he felt.

With that, the children and the leprechauns put together their plan to put on the performance of a lifetime, as promised.

An hour later, the leprechauns were finishing putting the chairs out for their audience, whilst the children looked on.

As the vampires started trailing in and sitting down, the leprechauns and children took their positions.

"Welcome to our little show!" Larry announced as he got on the stage. "We hope you find it very entertaining."

"Get on with it!" one of the vampires jeered.

"Very well," Larry smiled. "Let the show commence."

Lucy and Luke got up on the stage and started playing their guitars and singing.

As they did so, Kelsey slowly increased the volume on the loud speaker until it was as high as it could go. The vampires started cursing and screaming. It was too loud. They put their hands over their ears and tried to move, but the super glue on the chairs was doing its job.

Larry and Jonathan high-fived.

"Now!" Jonathan screamed as he and the leprechauns ran out and threw water balloons at the vampires.

The vampires screamed in pain, for it wasn't just any water, it was holy water.

Whilst this was going on, Kelsey and Tara crept onto the stage to get into position.

"Ready?" Tara asked. Kelsey nodded. "Aim and fire." Tara pointed at the vampires.

Tara shot arrows from her crossbow and Kelsey shot tranquiliser darts each one reaching its target.

The vampires screamed in terror and then some turned to dust and the rest fell into a deep slumber.

Silence descended on the land and then the leprechauns cheered.

The council finished the tranquilised vampires off with a swift stake to the heart and everyone heaved a sigh of relief.

"We must go!" Larry stated urgently. "You must get our amulet and be off to the next land."

"Relax!" Jonathan said. "We defeated the vampires, we should celebrate."

"No time!" Larry replied. "You still have so much to do!"

Tara put a calming hand on Jonathan's shoulder. "He's right. We can celebrate when this is all over."

Jonathan nodded, knowing that Tara was right.

"Where is the amulet?" he asked Larry.

Larry pointed to his very own pot of gold. "In there."

The children looked in the pot and saw one gold piece that looked more sparkly than the rest. Jonathan fished it out and put it in the satchel with the other amulets.

"Thank you, Larry! We couldn't have done this without you," Jonathan said as he hugged Larry.

Larry then sniffled and hugged Tara and Kelsey. "No, thank you all. We never would have got rid of the vampires if it hadn't been for you."

"How very touching!" a smooth voice came from behind them.

They whirled around just in time to see Thorn grab Tara.

"Tara!" Jonathan screamed. "Let her go!" he demanded.

"No, I don't think I will. Consider this payback for murdering my friends." Thorn lowered his mouth and sunk his teeth into Tara's neck. Tara whimpered as the others looked on in horror.

"Now, you have 24 hours to decide whether you want her to die or to become a vampire. After that, the choice no longer exists and she dies. Once you have made your decision, do let me know and you can return my amulets at the same..."

Thorn suddenly went slack and Jonathan looked around to see Larry blasting magic at Thorn until he was in a deep sleep.

"You must hurry to the next land!" Larry told Jonathan. "I will keep Tara safe in my house. You can get a spell from Witch Town to restore her."

"What about Thorn?" Jonathan asked.

"We can send him back to the Vampire Kingdom. Now..." Larry moved his hands in a circular pattern, producing the finest rainbow Jonathan had ever seen. "Step into the rainbow and it will take you to where you need to be. Take care, both of you."

Jonathan and Kelsey took one last look at the leprechauns and Tara and stepped gingerly into the rainbow.

CHAPTER 13

GREMLIN'S SCRAP VILLAGE

Jonathan and Kelsey landed in the next land with an unceremonious THUMP!

"Ouch!" Kelsey cried, rubbing her bottom.

"Something's not right," Jonathan said, looking around.

Kelsey looked around her and realised that Jonathan was right. Everywhere was dirty and dank and they were surrounded by scrap metal. Little creatures came whizzing past them so fast that they almost fell over again.

"We're not in Witch Town, are we?" Kelsey asked in dismay.

Jonathan shook his head, glumly. How were they going to rescue Tara now?

"Well, we need to find out where we are!" Kelsey stated resolutely. "The sooner we get the amulet from here, the sooner we can get to Witch Town."

They started exploring this new land and saw some little creatures playing in a car wreckage yard and destroying the cars.

"Hey, stop that!" Jonathan shouted.

"What's it to you?" one of the creatures asked rudely.

"Why would you break that car?" Jonathan demanded to know.

"Because we're in a yard for wrecking cars!" it pointed at the sign. "And that's what gremlins do, so there!" It stuck its tongue out at Jonathan.

"Gremlins?" Jonathan and Kelsey said in hushed tones.

"We're not gonna get anything out of them!" Jonathan pointed at the gremlins, who had gone back to destroying the car.

"So, what now?" Kelsey asked, worriedly.

Jonathan shook his head. He didn't know and he didn't have Tara there to help, although he didn't know how her strength would help anyway. Hang on a moment, that was it.

"Kels, I've got an idea. What if you try to listen to the gremlins' thoughts and we might find out where the amulet is?"

Kelsey looked excited and nodded. She screwed her face up with concentration and tried listening. All she could hear, though, was a lot of noise. There was so much chatter in her head that she was starting to get a headache.

"It's no use, Jon," she shook her head. "There's too much noise."

Jonathan looked as frustrated as she felt.

"C'mon," he nodded ahead of them. "Let's see if we can find somewhere quieter."

The children walked and walked, but all they could see was scrap metal and gremlins making so much noise.

They were about to give up when they saw a little pink Beetle that looked like it hadn't been touched by anyone. They ran to the car and got in.

"That's better." Jonathan breathed a sigh of relief at the quiet. "Now, how do we find the amulet?"

Kelsey shrugged, looking despondent.

"Cheer up, Kels. We'll find it."

Kelsey gave Jonathan a weak smile before bursting into tears.

Jonathan wrapped his arms around her and gave her the best hug a big brother could give. After a few minutes, Kelsey pulled away.

"I'm sorry, Jon. I just don't..." she stopped and listened.

"What is it?" Jonathan asked.

"Shhh!" came the reply.

Jonathan waited patiently, taking the time to really look at his sister. This quest had taken its toll on her and she was far more serious now. She was also the bravest of them all, for she was so young and yet so ready to do the right thing to save everybody.

"Jonathan!" Kelsey clicked her fingers.

"Sorry, I was miles away," Jonathan replied sheepishly.

"I just heard a gremlin, on his own out there. He was really angry, because all the other gremlins voted for him to be the protector, but he doesn't want to be the protector."

"Protector of what?" Jonathan interrupted.

Kelsey looked more and more excited.

"The amulet!" She grinned. "He's got it hidden in something called cargo!"

Jonathan hugged his sister. "That must be a cargo hold. They have them on planes. I think we passed an aircraft hangar on the way here."

Unable to believe their luck, the children got ready to climb out of the car, when they saw their worst nightmare. There stood Thorn, with their dad and a whole battalion of gremlins.

"Well, what do we have here?" Thorn sneered. "Just the people I was looking for. Time for me to get what's mine and for you to die."

Some of the gremlins sniggered.

Jonathan sat very still and made his thoughts crystal clear.

Kels, we need to get out of here!

"Huh?" Kelsey jumped.

"What's the matter, little girl?" Thorn asked. "No more tricks up your sleeves to thwart me?"

Kelsey thought that was very silly, because she wasn't wearing sleeves, but wisely shook her head and listened to Jonathan.

If I pick you up, we can make a run for it. Jonathan continued.

But Jon, I don't want to be picked up and we'll never make it. You know how fast Thorn and the gremlins are.

Jonathan replied. *I know, but we have no choice, it's our only chance. We'll pretend to surrender and then run.*

Kelsey gave an imperceptible nod and Jonathan spoke to Thorn. "Okay, we'll come with you," he grumbled. "But we don't have the amulets. We left them with Tara."

"Very well, boy," Thorn smiled sinisterly. "We'll go back for them."

Jonathan nodded glumly as he helped Kelsey out of the car.

The gremlins looked on eagerly and their father just cowered in Thorn's presence.

"I hope you're all happy!" Jonathan shouted to more sniggers. Jonathan went to pick Kelsey up.

"What are you doing?" Thorn asked incredulously.

"She's tired and she whinges very loudly when she's tired," Jonathan told him. "But if you'd rather..."

As if to prove Jonathan's point, Kelsey wailed, "I wanna go home!"

"Oh, very well!" Thorn said, irritated. "But be quick about it!"

"Of course!" Jonathan said smoothly and picked Kelsey up, thankful for all the times she'd made him play Princesses and he'd had to carry her, and then started walking towards the aircraft hangar.

"Hey, boy!" Thorn roared after him, "You're going the wrong way!"

Jonathan ignored him and started walking faster and faster until he was running!

Thorn raced after him. "You'll never outrun me, boy!" Thorn looked amused.

"Maybe not, but I'll give it a go!" Jonathan picked up speed and shoved gremlins behind him to slow Thorn down.

He could still hear Thorn and the gremlins coming up behind him, but they were starting to sound quieter. Jonathan looked behind him and saw they were all far behind him. And as he looked where he was going, he realised he was going so fast that everything he passed was blurry. Grinning to himself, he sped on until Thorn, the gremlins and his father were no longer in view.

Reaching the hangar, Jonathan set Kelsey down.

"Wow, Jon!" Kelsey said breathlessly and looking a bit green. "I guess we know what your power is."

Jonathan laughed. "I guess we do. Now, let's find this amulet!"

They walked into the hangar and saw two planes standing there.

"Which one do you think it's in?" Kelsey asked.

"I don't know. Why don't we look in one each and we can think to each other when we find it?"

"Okay. How will we know where to look?"

"The gremlin said it was in the cargo hold, so we start there."

"What's a cargo hold?" Kelsey asked.

After Jonathan had explained to Kelsey what a cargo hold was, they each stepped onto a plane. Kelsey took the one on the left and Jonathan took the one on the right.

Jonathan looked in crates and under sheets for anything that might be the amulet. He knew that Thorn would catch up with them soon and they needed to find the amulet. He kicked a crate in frustration, when he heard speaking.

Jon, I've found it! Kelsey thought to him. *You need to come here, now!*

Realising Kelsey sounded scared, Jonathan ran to her plane and got on just in time to see Thorn and the gremlins advancing on them.

"Sit down, Kels!" Jonathan ordered.

"What are you doing?" Kelsey did what he asked.

"I'm flying us out of here!"

"You've never flown a plane before!" Kelsey screamed.

Jonathan looked at Kelsey and hoped that he'd picked something up from all those films he had watched.

"Hold on!" he yelled as he turned on the ignition.

The plane started moving and gremlins started diving out of the way.

"Jonathan!" Kelsey screamed, as Thorn was getting closer.

Jonathan nodded and pulled the yoke, lifting the plane into the air and almost knocking Thorn over.

Jonathan laughed and whooped as they flew over an angry Thorn and Kelsey breathed a sigh of relief. Next stop: Witch Town.

CHAPTER 14

WITCH TOWN

"Look!" shouted Kelsey over the engine.

Jonathan looked where she was pointing and saw a green shimmery light.

"That must be Witch Town," he replied.

He started the slow descent, hoping that he didn't crash the plane. As the plane reached the ground, it jolted and bumped them until finally it came to a stop with a shudder.

Breathing a sigh of relief, Jonathan and Kelsey walked down the steps and stepped onto this new, wondrous land.

"Stay close to me, Kels," Jonathan held his hand out for her. This land was very mysterious and scary and Jonathan didn't want to lose Kelsey the way he'd lost Tara and Charlie. He knew deep down that what happened to them both wasn't his fault, but it didn't stop him from feeling guilty.

Kelsey held his hand and stood closely to him.

"How will we know who is good and evil? What if we meet a witch like in Hansel and Gretel and she wants to eat us?"

"It'll be fine! We'll be fine!" Jonathan said, trying to convince himself, as well as Kelsey. "Let's find this witch called Ash."

They walked along the cottages, happy that none were made of sweets, and noticed that each cottage had a name on it. Looking closely for the cottage that said Ash, they almost bumped into a witch.

"Oh, excuse me," stammered Jonathan, for this witch was very beautiful.

"It is of no matter," she replied regally. "You were lost deep in thought. What is troubling you?"

"We're looking for a witch named Ash," Jonathan replied.

"Jon?" Kelsey whimpered quietly.

"Not now, Kels!" Jonathan interrupted. "We don't want to be rude."

The witch gave a tinkling laugh that sounded like bells at Christmas.

"That's quite alright. How fortuitous that we bumped into each other. I am Ashleigh, but I much prefer Ash."

"You're Ash?" Jonathan gazed at this vision in front of him.

"Of course." she replied. "Let's go into my cottage."

As they walked to Ash's cottage, Kelsey tried pulling on Jonathan's hand, but he held firm and half dragged her to the cottage.

Once they arrived at the cottage, Ash opened the door and let them all in. "Please do make yourselves at home, I must prepare for our ritual."

"Don't you mean spells." Kelsey asked.

"Ah, yes," Ash looked thoughtful, a funny gleam appearing in her eye.

She snapped her fingers and a cage of vines wound its way around the children.

"Yes, you'll do very nicely in there, whilst I sort out my ritual!"

"Oh, brilliant! Another cage!" Jonathan kicked the vines, crossly.

"I did try to tell you that there was something strange about her." Kelsey reminded him. "She had some very bad thoughts."

"I know." Jonathan sighed. "I should have listened. I'm sorry, Kels."

Kelsey hugged Jonathan. "It's okay. But how are we getting out of here?"

Jonathan looked for a weakness in the vines, but they looked like they could hold King Kong in, so they didn't stand a chance.

"Why are you doing this, Ash?" Jonathan yelled.

"Are you going to eat us?" Kelsey asked, fearfully.

"Okay, let's have some proper introductions," Ash said cheerfully, as though she hadn't trapped them in a cage. "My name is Tilly. And of course I'm not going to eat you!" she replied.

Kelsey sighed in relief.

"I'm just going to kill you and sell your bodies to Thorn!"

"What?" Jonathan roared, as Kelsey started to cry. "You can't be serious! And this cottage says it belongs to Ash."

"Oh! I'm deadly serious," Tilly laughed. "Yes, this cottage is Ash's, I'm just borrowing it."

Jonathan couldn't think of anything else to say, so he clung to Kelsey and prayed for a miracle. He wasn't one for prayer usually, but he figured that if ever there was a time to start, it was when they were trapped in a vine cage about to die.

"Now, which one of you would like to go first?" Tilly asked, as if she were asking about the weather. "Now, come on!" a bit more crossly. "One of you has to..."

BANG!

The door slammed open and Tilly went flying across the room. A man entered the cottage, furious and foreboding.

"Ash!" Tilly said breathlessly. "A pleasure as always!"

"You have precisely 10 seconds to leave my house, before I make your worst nightmare a reality!" the man threatened quietly with cold fury.

"Of course!" Tilly replied. "I'll just be on my way," she remarked cheerfully, waving at the children as she sped out of there.

The man rubbed his temple and waved his hand to rid the cottage of the vines.

"I'm Asher. You can call me Ash if you want," he told them grumpily.

Looking at him, they saw he had a scar running all the way down his face and the wildest hair they had ever seen.

"You really need to be more careful," Ash, continued, ignoring their stares. "I'd have thought you would have learned by now that appearances can be deceiving."

Jonathan could feel himself going red and mumbled an apology.

Ash nodded at him and changed the subject. "Now, Larry got a message to me!"

"You know Larry?" Jonathan interrupted.

"Yes, of course! Larry has filled me in on everything that has been going on and it seems you've been making messes all over the place."

"We didn't mean to!" Kelsey cried.

Ash's face softened. "I know, Kelsey, but we now need to fix the mess, you see?"

Kelsey nodded tearfully.

"Right, first thing's first," Ash said, clapping his hands together. "These are the ingredients we need for the potions and where to find them and you are going to get them!" Ash pointed at Jonathan and Kelsey, handing them a piece of paper that materialised. "And please do watch out for dragons! The last thing we need is you two disappearing too!"

Jonathan nodded firmly, determined not to let Ash down.

Once outside, they decided to come up with a plan to avoid the dragons.

"If I run really fast around them and you make them think they need to go in the opposite direction, then hopefully we can confuse them a bit," Jonathan said thoughtfully.

Kelsey nodded, eager to get the herbs and get back.

For the next hour, Jonathan and Kelsey tricked the dragons and collected herbs, until they only had one herb left to find.

"Okay, we need echinacea. It's purple." Jonathan said.

"Look!" Kelsey shouted. "Is that it?"

Jonathan ran to where Kelsey was pointing and nodded. He quickly added them to the pile of herbs and motioned to Kelsey that they should return.

After a few wrong turns, they made it back to Ash's house and Ash set to work.

He knew that Tara didn't have much longer, so he started her potion first.

He stirred in all the herbs he needed and started chanting in a strange language.

"Fetch me a vial!" he ordered Jonathan.

Jonathan did as he asked and Ash transferred the potion to the vial. He waved his hand in a circular motion and the potion started glowing a very deep red.

When it stopped glowing, he placed the vial down and cleared the table. Waving his hands over the table, a figure started to appear. As the figure started to become more solid, Jonathan realised it was Tara.

"Now, you must get Tara to drink the potion. She must drink all of it and she will be restored."

Jonathan nodded and held Tara in a seated position. Opening her mouth, he poured the vial down her throat. He waited for what seemed like an eternity and suddenly Tara spluttered.

"Jonathan!" she gasped and flung her arms around him, kissing him.

Jonathan wrapped his arms around Tara, so relieved she was okay and kissed her back. They stepped away from each other with embarrassment and Kelsey rolled her eyes.

"Teenagers!" she muttered under her breath.

Still holding hands, Tara and Jonathan turned to Ash. "Thank you so much." they said gratefully.

Ash nodded and made a start on Charlie's potion. There didn't seem to be much difference, Jonathan thought, except this one glowed teal instead of red.

"Okay, because Charlie isn't here and he is trapped in a very powerful binding spell, Tara will need to drink this potion as well. As long as they share DNA, it will work."

Tara nodded and started drinking the potion whilst Ash chanted his spell and danced around her.

"Eugh, that was disgusting!" Tara coughed.

"Why isn't anything happening?" she asked a few minutes later. Ash was about to respond when they heard a clap of thunder and smoke rose from the ground.

When the smoke had cleared, there stood Charlie and Sparks.

"What're you all looking at?" Charlie asked.

Everyone laughed and hugged him, while Sparks ran around them all, licking them.

"Now, I must do the potion for your father," Ash said solemnly. "I must have no interruptions for it requires complete concentration."

The children sat quietly and Tara held onto a wriggling Charlie to stop him from disrupting Ash's work.

Soon, they heard Ash sigh. "It is almost done! All it needs to do is cool and turn the colour of fire. Now, let's eat!" Ash conjured an enormous feast for them all, including all of their favourite foods. The children ate greedily, feeling as though they hadn't eaten for months.

A ping sounded, announcing that the potion was finished and Ash went to pick it up. He handed the potion to Jonathan and gave him two pieces of paper.

"These are the two spells you will need," he told the children. "The one in your left hand contains the spell to free your father.

This must be done in Thorn's lair in the Vampire Kingdom. You have to capture your father and make him drink the potion whilst the rest of you stake 12 vampires around him."

"How can I read this?" Jonathan asked.

"The paper is enchanted to show the language of the reader."

"How are we going to get 12 vampires to surround him?" Tara asked sensibly.

"You will find a way. Although, Jonathan stood in Thorn's lair with his father should offer the vampires the proper incentive." Ash then continued. "The second your father has drunk the last drop, you must recite the spell. It is imperative you do it in this order or the spell won't work and your father will be lost forever."

Kelsey gasped and Jonathan nodded. "We'll get it right?"

Ash smiled sadly and continued. "Do not be over confident. That will be Thorn's downfall, don't let it be yours."

Jonathan nodded seriously and squeezed Kelsey's hand.

"The spell in your right hand is the one to find the amulet. To do this you must go deep into the woods and recite the spell, then a portal will appear. You must enter the portal and answer the riddle the oldest witch asks of you."

"The oldest witch?" Charlie interrupted.

"Yes, the oldest of our kind. Once you have answered the riddle correctly, she will give you the amulet. Then you must recite the spell again and a new portal will take you to the next land. Now, you must leave and I wish you all the best of luck."

The children all hugged Ash and said goodbye to him and made their way into the woods.

"How far into the woods do we have to go?" Kelsey asked fearfully.

"I think here is probably far enough. It's very dark." Tara replied.

"Okay, Tara, you're more articulate than we are, so you should recite the spell," Jonathan handed the spell to her.

Tara nodded nervously. "Door open to warriors four." her voice sounding out the words clearly.

The children looked at each other.

Had Tara said it right?

"Look!" Charlie pointed.

The others followed where he was pointing and the clearing in front of them started glowing. The glow grew brighter and brighter until they were standing in front of a portal.

"Shall we?" Jonathan gestured and they all stepped through.

A serene elderly witch stood in front of them.

"Are you ready?" the witch spoke. At least, they thought she spoke, because they couldn't see her lips move.

The children nodded.

"If you get the answer wrong, you will remain in the void with me."

Again the children nodded, feeling more and more nervous. There was something about this witch that wasn't quite right.

The witch gazed at them and recited the riddle. "What can run but never walks, has a mouth but never talks, has a head but never weeps, has a bed but never sleeps."

The children looked at each other worriedly, but Tara sat down to think about the riddle. She went over the problem in her head until she shouted "I've got it!" startling everyone.

"What is your answer child?" the witch asked, her lips twisting in an unnatural fashion.

Not noticing, Tara asked excitedly, "It's a river, isn't it?"

"Well done, you have done well." The witch handed the amulet to Tara. "It would have been nice to have some company!" she grabbed at Sparks, who leaped out of the way.

Jonathan drew his sword, as the witch sneered at him.

Jonathan looked in horror as the witch grew and her face contorted into a grotesque monster!

"Hurry!" he screamed, swinging his sword at the witch.

Tara recited the spell as quickly as she could and the portal opened.

"Jump!" Jonathan yelled, grabbing Kelsey.

All the children heard was a bloodcurdling scream as they jumped through the portal.

CHAPTER 15

HAUNTED HOUSE

The children screamed as they landed with a thud on a hard wooden floor.

"Where are we?" asked Tara.

Jonathan shrugged looking around him. "It looks like a house of some sort."

"Ouch!" yelled Charlie. Something had hit him on his arm.

"Look out!" Jonathan shouted, as a tea cup flew across the room.

"Everyone, get down!" Tara screamed as a drawer flew towards them.

As they crouched down, they heard a wailing moan.

"I don't like the sound of that," Kelsey whimpered, with Sparks cuddling up to her.

"I know," Jonathan replied, "but we need to find the amulet. If we take one floor at a time and stick together then we should find it soon enough."

"But Jonathan," Tara spoke up, "we'll find it faster if we split up and take a floor each."

Jonathan looked worriedly at Kelsey.

"She's right, Jon," Kelsey told him. "I'm scared, but if we find the amulet quicker, I'll be scared for less time."

Jonathan didn't like it, but he knew that the sooner they left this place, the better he would feel, so he nodded. "But if anyone gets into trouble, scream."

Everyone agreed, knowing that they probably wouldn't have any control over their screaming.

"Okay, Tara, you check the attic. I think I saw some stairs to one."

Tara nodded and went in the direction Jonathan pointed.

"Charlie, you stay on this floor. Use your x-ray vision if you need to."

Charlie saluted Jonathan and wandered into the next room.

"Kels, you take the floor below us and take Sparks with you for protection."

Sparks puffed his chest out with pride.

"What about you, Jon?" Kelsey asked.

"A house like this is bound to have a basement."

Kelsey and Jonathan split up and Jonathan crept down to the basement. It was very quiet down there, but it didn't feel peaceful.

"Jonathan!" a voice whispered in his ear.

Jonathan whirled around, but there was nothing there.

"Jonathan!" the voice came louder.

"Who's there?" Jonathan shouted, drawing his sword.

"It's only me, Jonathan!" Jonathan turned and saw Tara.

"Tara!" he said in relief. "You're supposed to be…"

A pirate came up behind Tara and thrust his sword through her shoulder blades.

"NO!" Jonathan screamed, as Tara crumpled to the ground and the pirate disappeared.

He ran to her and went to hold her but she vanished.

"What the…" Jonathan muttered, still crying.

Suddenly, he heard a piercing scream coming from upstairs and he ran towards the sound.

Meanwhile, Kelsey and Sparks had gone downstairs and they found the kitchen.

"Okay, Sparks, let's see if there's some food here for you before we look for the amulet."

Sparks nodded eagerly and then jumped into Kelsey's arms when they heard cackling.

"Wh-wh-who's there?" Kelsey stammered.

The cackling grew louder as a ghost appeared before them. No - not a ghost - a poltergeist as it started throwing pots and pans at them.

"Hey!" Kelsey shouted as she ducked just in time.

Sparks flew away from Kelsey and started snorting fire at the poltergeist, but it was no use, because the flames just went straight through it and it laughed even more.

Kelsey looked around her for things to defend herself with and threw knives and forks at the poltergeist, but they just went through it.

Frustrated, she picked up a wooden chopping board and threw it.

The poltergeist laughed as the chopping board went through it, but both Kelsey and the poltergeist watched as the chopping board hit the loose wire dangling down the wall.

A spark suddenly came from the wire and the poltergeist screamed and floated away as fast as it could.

"Yay, Sparks, we did it!" Kelsey hugged Sparks while he nuzzled her neck.

That's when they heard the most awful scream.

"Quick, Sparks! I think it came from over there."

Kelsey and Sparks ran towards the scream.

Whilst Jonathan and Kelsey had been fighting, Charlie started searching on his floor. He entered one of the bedrooms and started rummaging through the drawers.

He heard a giggle behind him and whirled around. An apparition appeared before him. She looked like a girl of no more than 8 or 9. Charlie stood there, transfixed.

As a 7 year old boy, he didn't much like girls, but there was something about this girl.

"Are you an angel?" Charlie asked.

The little girl giggled again and put her finger to her lips, looking behind him.

Charlie looked behind him and a demon appeared and grabbed him. The demon looked to be the same age as the little girl, but he was strong.

Charlie yelled and struggled, but the demon's grip only grew stronger. Charlie could feel himself going limp when bright floating lights entered the room and swirled around him and the demon. Charlie thought this meant he was passing out but, to his surprise, the demon dropped him and fell down as the lights started moving faster around him.

Charlie suddenly heard Tara scream. He knew it was her from all the times he'd stuck frogs in her bed. Without a second thought, Charlie ran towards his sister.

Tara, meanwhile, had found the stairs to the attic. They looked a bit rickety, but she couldn't see any other way up. So she tentatively put her foot on the first step and held her breath. It creaked slightly, but nothing happened, so she started climbing the stairs, slowly.

She had almost reached the top when the step underneath her gave way and she felt herself falling. Screaming, she flailed about; trying to grab onto something, but there was nothing there. She shut her eyes, waiting for the inevitable impact. When nothing happened, she cautiously opened her eyes and saw that she was floating. Looking up, she saw a beautiful angel, surrounded by a bright white light, raising her arms and Tara felt herself rise up towards the attic.

Tumbling into the attic, she tried looking at the angel, but the light was too bright.

"Am I dead?" she gasped. "Am I in heaven?"

The angel looked down on her. "No, you are very much alive," she chuckled.

Tara tried looking around the attic, but the light made it very difficult for her to see.

She was about to ask the angel if she knew where the amulet was when the others ran into the room.

"Tara!" they all yelled in unison, piling on top of her.

"I'm fine," she laughed when they got off her. "How did you all get up here?"

"We jumped over the missing step!" Charlie replied proudly.

"Oh, Charlie, you could've been hurt." She hugged her brother.

After their initial relief that Tara was okay, they noticed that the room was brighter and there was a being in the room with them.

Jonathan was immediately on his guard, but Tara put her hand on his arm.

"It's okay, she's an angel. She saved my life."

Jonathan nodded and lowered his sword.

The angel looked at them all, knowing how much they'd been through and how much was yet to come. She pointed at a chest in the middle of the room.

"What you wish for is in there."

The children went up to the chest and Jonathan used his sword to open it. They'd had enough frights today and they didn't need anymore. Flipping the chest open, they saw a green glow and realised it was the amulet.

Tara looked worriedly behind them, because they could hear moaning and groaning coming from below and it was getting closer.

"You must all hurry!" the angel urged them. "I can hold them off for you."

"Thank you," Tara said softly.

The angel nodded. "Before you go, you must know that the next land is Pixie Land."

Kelsey looked excited to be meeting pixies.

"Be careful when you get there." the angel continued. "Pixie Land is beautiful, but it is also enchanted and very dangerous. The pixies love dancing, but if you start dancing, you won't be able to stop. Here is an elixir to use in emergencies and will put a stop to any dancing and here are some ear plugs so that the music will be muffled."

She handed these to the children and they put them in their pockets.

"Now," she moved them to the wall at the end of the attic and moved an ancient painting to reveal a tunnel.

As they looked into the tunnel, the angel's light dimmed and Tara gasped as she turned around.

"Mum?" she asked quietly.

"Yes, my child," her mother replied. "I have been with you every step of the way and I am so proud of you and Charlie."

Tara cried as she hugged her mother.

"I can't follow you any further on this quest," she ruffled Charlie's hair as he hugged her, tears streaming down his face. "But know that I have faith that you can do what needs to be done." She looked at Jonathan and Kelsey. "All of you."

"Why can't you come with us?" Tara cried, not ready to let go.

"I must stay behind to give you time to get to Pixie Land, I'll be fine." she told a stricken Tara and Charlie. "Now, you must go quickly. I love you both very much and I will see you again."

She bundled the children into the tunnel, giving Tara and Charlie one last hug and then replaced the painting.

The children heard the sounds of a commotion and Tara cried as Jonathan pulled her and Charlie gently through the tunnel to Pixie Land.

Chapter 16

Pixie Land

The children crept through the tunnel as fast and quietly as they could, not looking back for fear they were being followed.

They jumped out of the tunnel when they reached the end and Tara collapsed to the ground, sobbing. Jonathan didn't know what to do, so he held her whilst she cried.

Eventually, she pulled away and wiped her eyes. Looking around she noticed it was night time and there were pretty little fairy lights decorating the trees.

"I guess this is Pixie Land then." she said to the others.

"It's pretty." Kelsey remarked.

Jonathan nodded and led the others nervously into the woods. The further they went, the more lights were strung up and they could hear the sound of movement. Jonathan stopped suddenly, causing Charlie to bump into him.

"Ow!" Charlie said crossly.

"Sorry, Charlie, but look!" Jonathan pointed to a spot in the woods where pixies were laughing and dancing.

Jonathan, Tara and Kelsey looked mesmerised, but Charlie remembered what his mother had said and quickly put in his earplugs. He watched in horror as everyone else started dancing. Everyone except Sparks, who appeared to be immune.

"Come on Charlie, come and dance with us!" Tara swayed to the music as Sparks tried to pull on his jeans. Tara nudged Sparks away angrily. "Stop trying to spoil our fun!"

Charlie was on the verge of tears, but knew he needed to get the elixir that was in Tara's pocket. As he pondered how to get the elixir, he noticed Tara had moved further away and some angry pixies were dancing in a circle around him and Sparks.

How was he going to get to Tara?

An idea struck him and he whispered his idea to Sparks. Sparks leaped over the pixies and started running through the pixies in the woods. Charlie started dancing and pretending the music was affecting him so that the pixies surrounding him would go after Sparks. Sure enough they nodded at Charlie and started chasing after Sparks, who kept one step ahead of them.

Now the coast was clear, Charlie kept dancing and moving towards Tara. "Tara, do you have any sweets?" he asked.

Tara looked surprised and shook her head.

"Could you check your pockets, please?" Charlie continued in a whining voice that he knew Tara hated.

Tara turned out her pockets and pulled out the elixir. "Sorry Charlie, I've got nothing except this little drink."

Charlie nodded. "That's okay, I'll have some of that. All this dancing is thirsty work."

Tara chuckled and handed him the elixir.

Charlie pretended to drink some and then handed it back to Tara. "Here, have some. It's delicious!"

Tara shrugged and took a sip of the elixir. Immediately she stopped dancing. "Thanks Charlie," she hugged her brother awkwardly. "Let's get the others."

Tara and Charlie ran to Jonathan and Kelsey.

"Why aren't you dancing?" Jonathan asked crossly.

"We got thirsty," Tara answered, handing Jonathan the elixir. Jonathan took a quick sip and realised what he was doing. "Here, Kels. Have a sip."

Kelsey shook her head. "Don't want to!"

Jonathan looked over Kelsey's head helplessly at Tara.

"Sorry about this, Kelsey!"

"Wha-" Kelsey started as Tara lifted her up like a sack of potatoes. Kelsey kicked and struggled, but Tara held firm. Sitting her on a tree stump at the edge of the woods, Jonathan fed her the elixir. Kelsey looked down at her feet, embarrassed, mumbling "Thanks."

"No problem!" Charlie replied, feeling more cheerful now everyone was back to normal.

Tara hugged Kelsey. "What do we do now?" she asked, watching the pixies chase after Sparks, who appeared to be having the time of his life.

"Well first we do this!" Jonathan turned the music off. Immediately the pixies stopped chasing Sparks and whirled around to glare at the children. They advanced towards the children. "Great plan, Jon!" Kelsey said sarcastically. "Now what?" Jonathan looked perplexed, he hadn't thought that far ahead.

"What's the big idea?" one of the pixies demanded.

"We're sorry," Kelsey apologised.

"I'm Kelsey and this is Jonathan, Tara and Charlie."

"And I'm Penny, the head pixie. Why did you turn our music off?"

"We need your help!" begged Kelsey. "We've come so far already and we need to stop Thorn getting the amulets, so we need the amulet that's here."

Kelsey was close to tears because everything was very overwhelming.

"Hmm," Penny looked at the children. "Very well, I will help you. Follow me."

The children, Sparks and many of the pixies followed Penny into a glade in the centre of the woods. There was a stone in the middle, with the amulet embedded in it and a strange glow around it. Penny pointed at the stone and said, "If you can free the amulet from the stone, it is yours. If you manage this, you must walk 3 miles north and climb a ladder over the soft wall to the Giant Village. Do you understand?"

The children nodded their understanding.

"How nice of you to lead me to another amulet," a voice they had come to dread appeared behind them.

The pixies, panicking, started to scatter.

"Run for your lives!" one of the pixies screamed. Unfortunately, Penny wasn't fast enough and Thorn plucked her off the ground.

"Now, isn't this interesting!" he said smoothly. "You now have a choice. You can hand over all the amulets including this one," he pointed at the amulet in the stone. "Or" he continued. "I can feed on dear old Penny here." Thorn knew that the children wouldn't let an innocent die, so the amulets were as good as his.

"Don't worry about me!" Penny screamed. "Only one who has grown and evolved can get the amulet. You must hurry."

"Shut up, you little pest!" Thorn hissed angrily. "So, what's it to be?" he leered at Jonathan and Tara.

Jonathan was furious. There was no way he was letting Thorn win and was ready to charge at Thorn with his sword when Kelsey thought *stop*.

Thorn smirked. "You should listen to your sister."

Kelsey used all her effort to block Thorn from hearing what came next. *Everyone put your earplugs in and follow my instructions.*

The others did as Kelsey asked, leaving Thorn confused. "What the…"

"Alright Thorn, you win," Jonathan said, shoulders slumped in defeat.

"No tricks this time, boy?" he demanded.

Jonathan shook his head slowly, whilst Kelsey crept to the music box and turned the music on.

"What's happening?" Thorn screamed, as he started dancing against his will.

The children and the pixies started giggling as he shouted, "I'll kill you for this!"

"Not until you get out of this, you won't!" Jonathan laughed as he retrieved Penny from Thorn.

"Well done!" Penny gasped. "I really thought you were giving them to him."

"We would never do that," Tara said softly. "But we couldn't let him kill you either."

"I am very glad for that. You are true warriors."

The children all blushed at her compliment and Penny smiled at them. These children really didn't realise how special they all were.

"Okay, how do we get this amulet?" Jonathan asked.

"As I said before, only one who has grown and evolved can get the amulet."

The children looked at the stone, willing the amulet to show them who should retrieve it. "Well, we can't stand staring all day, let's take it in turns. First me, then Tara, then Kelsey and then Charlie."

"Why am I last?" Charlie grumbled.

"Because if we can't then you are our last hope!" Tara told him. Charlie seemed quite happy at that and nodded.

Jonathan went to the amulet and pulled at it. It wouldn't budge. He tried to get his sword to ease it off, but to no avail. "Your go!" he grumbled to Tara. Tara nodded and grabbed at the amulet, but it stayed stuck fast.

Tara huffed as she kept pulling on it, but the amulet wouldn't even move an inch for her.

Kelsey went up next and rolled up her sleeves. Well, she would have rolled up her sleeves, if she had sleeves. Running at the rock, she tried pushing it and pulling it as hard as she could but nothing would move this amulet.

"Your go," she said to Charlie, dejectedly.

Charlie looked at the others nervously as they all gave him looks of encouragement.

Marching up to the stone, he put his hand on the amulet and plucked the amulet out.

"You did it, Charlie!" Tara squealed and hugged her brother.

"I thought there'd be a bright light or something." Jonathan remarked, putting a hand on Charlie's shoulder.

"This isn't Excalibur!" Penny laughed. "Charlie has grown the most on your journey and the amulet recognised that."

"How have I grown?" Charlie put his hand above his head to see how tall he was.

Penny laughed, "Not that kind of grown. The kind that comes from within. Think back to who you were at the beginning of your journey and who you are now!"

Charlie looked at the others, who all nodded at him, including Kelsey. "Oh!" he said, understanding.

"What do we do about Thorn?" Jonathan asked, concern etched on his face.

"Don't worry! Our magic is very strong and powerful. He won't leave for some time. We can enlist help from the fairies, elves and leprechauns. We should have enough to portal him somewhere else."

"Thank you so much," Tara hugged Penny.

"You are very welcome, all of you," Penny said with tears rolling down her cheeks. "Now go! You must hurry!"

The children waved goodbye and ran as fast as they could to the wall hoping against hope that Penny was right.

Gasping, they reached the wall.

"It's like the wall to a bouncy castle!" Kelsey giggled.

"A lot taller though," Tara acknowledged.

"Well, shall we?" Jonathan gestured for everyone else to go ahead of him.

He took one last look at Pixie Land and started the long climb to Giant Village.

CHAPTER 17

THE GIANT VILLAGE

The children started the long climb up the ladder.

Jonathan was surprised at how sturdy it was, considering how rubbery the wall was. Still, they were having to move slowly and it was taking a long time.

"We'll never get there at this rate!" Jonathan grumbled, as he watched Kelsey and Charlie struggle up ahead.

"How much further?" Kelsey cried. "My feet hurt!"

"Mine too!" wailed Charlie, not to be outdone by Kelsey.

"Sparks!" Jonathan shouted to the little dragon.

Sparks flew up to him.

"Can you fly Kelsey and Charlie to the top for us?" Sparks nodded and went straight to Kelsey. Sparks didn't say this, but Kelsey was his favourite human ever. She gave him treats when the others weren't looking and she gave the best belly rubs. Putting his paws out for Kelsey, she grabbed on and he lifted her into the air. After a few seconds of fear, Kelsey started looking around. The world was very different from this height.

"What about me?" Charlie wailed.

"You're next, Charlie!" Jonathan reassured him.

Once Sparks had taken Kelsey to the top of the wall and made sure she was safe, he came back down for Charlie. Charlie grabbed at Sparks eagerly and almost fell, but Sparks caught him and lifted him up to safety.

Jonathan heaved a sigh of relief and continued up the ladder. He and Tara had made it halfway up the ladder, when Tara stopped.

"What's the matter?" Jonathan asked, worried.

"I'm sorry, Jonathan. I don't think I can go any further."

"Why?"

"I just looked down and saw how high up we are and now I've gone quite dizzy." Tara looked close to tears.

"Don't worry," Jonathan said. "I'm right here with you."

Tara looked at Jonathan fearfully.

"How do I get up to the top. Sparks can't carry me, I'm too heavy."

Jonathan looked at Tara and the ladder and thought for a moment.

"I've got it!" he exclaimed, almost making Tara fall off. "Sorry," he said sheepishly.

"What have you got?" Tara asked, feeling her panic growing larger.

"I'll put my arm around you and use my other hand to guide us up the ladder."

Tara attempted to nod as another wave of dizziness took over her.

Jonathan placed his arm firmly around Tara. "Is this okay?" he asked.

Again, Tara nodded and Jonathan placed his other hand on the ladder. Using his upper arm strength, Jonathan guided them both up the ladder. It was slow work, but gradually they started seeing the top of the wall.

"Come on, just a few more steps." Jonathan puffed as they finally reached the top.

"Now, just look at me, don't look down!" he said as they sat down.

"Thank you, Jonathan. I'm not usually that scared of heights, but..." Tara trailed off, looking around them.

"Where are Kelsey, Charlie and Sparks?" she asked puzzled.

Jonathan looked around and realised they were nowhere to be found.

Just about to shout for them, he turned and saw a big hand coming towards him and Tara. Jonathan and Tara did the only thing they could think of to do; they screamed.

"Put us down!" Tara screamed at the giant who was now carrying them away.

The giant merely guffawed and continued until he reached a huge cave. Entering the cave, he dropped Jonathan and Tara into a giant bowl, where Kelsey and Charlie were sitting looking bored.

"Kelsey! Charlie!" Jonathan gave them both a hug, followed by Tara.

"Geroff!" Charlie grumbled to both of them.

"Are you okay?" Jonathan asked Kelsey seriously.

Kelsey shrugged, "Sparks flew off, he'll get help."

Charlie scoffed at this, "Where is this help then?"

Kelsey was just about to retaliate when Jonathan realised they weren't in a bowl after all. "We're in a cauldron! This giant is planning on eating us!"

The children looked at each other in terror and started yelling and screaming as much as they could. The giant just looked at them and laughed.

Whilst all this was going on, Sparks had flown away. Kelsey was right, he was trying to find help and he knew just where to go. He'd heard of a giant called Tommy, who was always friendly to dragons. Now he just had to find him. Flying high, he looked all around him, until he saw a bookstore called 'Tommy's Tales.' Flying down, he entered the shop. A giant, reading his newspaper, looked up at the interruption.

"Ah, a customer. And what can I do for you, little fella?" the giant boomed.

Sparks started telling the giant what had gone on, but the giant interrupted. "Slow down, little guy. My dragon is a little rusty."

Sparks looked at him in amazement. It hadn't occurred to him that the giant might understand him. Which, upon thinking about it, he realised his plan hadn't been very well thought out.

"Let's start again. I'm Tommy and I own this shop. What's your name?"

Sparks told him and, after a bit of coaxing, told Tommy the whole story.

"So!" Tommy summarised. "Your friends have been kidnapped by an evil giant and you need help rescuing them."

Sparks nodded eagerly.

"Well, we'd better get started." Tommy rang a bell in his shop and within 5 minutes, half a dozen other giants entered.

Sparks looked around nervously, because he'd never been around this many giants before.

Tommy looked kindly at Sparks and then started the meeting, telling all the giants everything Sparks had told him.

"I think I know the giant you are talking about," a giant called Irina said. "He's called Malcolm and he is absolutely awful! What are we going to do?"

"I propose that we march up to his lair and take those children back from him. All in favour, raise your hands!" Tommy commanded.

The other giants reluctantly raised their hands, mentally preparing themselves for battle.

"Lead the way, Sparks!"

Sparks flew ahead of the giants as they marched along, until they reached Malcolms lair.

Tommy banged on the door. No one answered, so he banged again.

"What do you want?" Malcolm snarled as he opened the door. "I'm cooking dinner!"

"You have something that belongs to us!" Tommy boomed at Malcolm.

Malcolm sneered, "Well, why don't you come and get it?"

That was all it took for the giants to all wade in and start fighting. Malcolm's friends came out to join in and one giant went flying past Sparks.

Unnoticed by any of the giants, Sparks crept into Malcolms lair and saw the huge cauldron in the middle of the room. Flying up to it, he saw the children tied up in the cauldron.

"Oh Sparks, you came back!" Kelsey hugged Sparks and looked smugly at Charlie.

"What's going on out there?" Jonathan asked as Sparks shot flames at the ropes tying them up. "Sounds like an earthquake."

"I think that might be the help that Sparks went looking for, right Sparks?" Tara looked at the little dragon.

Sparks nodded eagerly and lifted Kelsey out of the cauldron. Then he went back for Charlie and let Tara and Jonathan use his tail as a rope to get out. The children were all so grateful to Sparks and gave him lots of extra pets and a couple of juicy apples.

"Where to now?" asked Tara. "We have no idea where the amulet is."

Jonathan was about to answer when Sparks started pulling at Jonathan's jeans. Jonathan knew better than to question Sparks by now and beckoned for the others to follow Sparks.

They all crept up the stairs in the cave and saw a chest in the middle of the room.

"Not another chest!" Charlie groaned.

The others laughed. "Come on, Charlie, let's find the amulet," Tara said.

They crept up to the chest and saw that it was full of gold. Gasping, Tara noticed the amulet was nestled neatly in with the gold. Grabbing it, she shouted, "Let's go!"

The children all ran down the stairs and out of Malcolms' lair.

Malcolm suddenly saw them. "Stop them!" he roared as he lunged for them. The children screamed, but Malcolm was tackled by one of the good giants.

"Go!" the giant shouted at them. "Run as fast as you can!"

Not needing to be told twice, the children and Sparks ran as fast as they could, until the giants were mere blips in the distance.

Slowing down, they looked around and realised they had reached the deep, dark wood and the entrance to the Vampires' Kingdom.

CHAPTER 18

THE VAMPIRES' KINGDOM

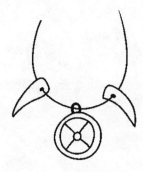

The children clung together as they crept into the deep, dark wood. Kelsey shivered. There was no sunlight, so it was cold as well as creepy. They kept going until they reached a clearing.

In the front of them were 3 paths, but only one could lead to Thorn's lair, where they knew the last amulet would be.

"Which path do we go down?" Kelsey asked.

"I don't know!" Jonathan answered, despairingly. "Maybe we could ask one of the vampires."

"I'm not sure that's the best idea," Tara said, looking fearfully at the vampires.

"How else are we going to…"

"Look!" Charlie shouted.

"Shh, Charlie!" Tara hissed.

"Sorry, but look!" Charlie whispered.

The children looked where he pointed and saw a green light glowing down on one of the paths.

"It could be a trap," Tara pointed out.

"Maybe, but what choice do we have? If we stick together we'll be alright," Jonathan said, sounding more confident than he felt.

Holding hands, with Sparks treading cautiously ahead of them, they walked down the green path. The vampires leered at them as they went past, but they ignored them. They hadn't attacked, so they must be under orders not to harm the children.

At the end of the path, they saw a damp cave with a sign outside saying Thorn's lair.

"This looks like a trap!" Tara said. The others agreed with her and sat down trying to come up with a plan.

"I know..." Kelsey started and then shook her head. That will never work!

"How about..." Tara thought out loud. "Mmm, maybe not."

"We could go and fight the vampires!" Charlie said, matter-of-factly.

"Oh, Charlie!" Tara ruffled his hair.

"I've got it!" Jonathan exclaimed. Everyone looked at him expectantly.

"We get captured!"

The others looked at Jonathan strangely.

"Jonathan, that's the last thing we want to happen," Tara interjected calmly.

"Wait, just hear me out!"

The children went quiet.

"We're probably going to get captured anyway, but we can use it to our advantage. Once Thorn has us, we can combine all our powers. So, Kelsey can repel Thorn's telepathy so he doesn't know what we're thinking. Charlie can locate the amulet and tell Kelsey, who'll tell us. Tara can use her strength to fight off the vampire guards holding us. Then I can run as fast as I can so the guards can't catch me. All the commotion will attract more vampires and I'll keep out running them until I stop suddenly and Tara and I can stake each vampire. I reckon Thorn will just sit and watch, until he needs to join in."

Jonathan looked at the others expectantly.

"But Jonathan," Kelsey poked timidly. "Remember what Ash said. We need to stake 12 vampires around Dad, give him the potion and recite the spell."

Jonathan nodded his head. Much as he hated to admit it, Kelsey had a point.

"Okay," he said, after some thought. "Tara can grab Dad, whilst I run around the vampires. I can stake the 12 vampires and Kelsey and Charlie can force the potion down him and then we all stand around him to recite the spell."

"Jonathan," Kelsey interjected again. Jonathan sighed.

"Yes, Kels."

"Thorn probably won't sit still whilst all this is going on, which will make things harder and we need to get the amulet."

"Can I make a suggestion?" Tara asked.

Jonathan nodded and gestured for her to continue.

"Why don't I knock the guards out, then Jonathan can pick me up and run at Thorn at full speed, so I can punch him and knock him out. Then we continue with Jonathan's plan, which is a good one." Jonathan blushed, pleased with Tara's praise.

The children sat for a few more minutes, working out the details of their plan. Once they were confident enough, they walked up to the lair.

"Who goes there?" a guard demanded.

"Oh, I'm sorry," Tara tittered. "We were looking for Thorn!"

"And you've found him!" The other guard leered at them. "Grab them!"

The guards went to grab the children and the children pretended to put up a fight, but let the guards capture them.

Kelsey stopped struggling enough to concentrate and repel Thorn's telepathy.

Meanwhile, Charlie looked around as they entered Thorn's lair and immediately saw the amulet around Thorn's neck. He told Kelsey, who told Tara and Jonathan.

Giving a slight nod of the head, Jonathan gave Tara her signal. She elbowed one guard and kicked the other and then cracked their heads together until they slumped to the ground.

"What is the meaning of this!" Thorn thundered.

Tara nodded at Jonathan, who picked her up and ran full speed at Thorn. Tara punched Thorn and Thorn fell back into his chair, a look of shock still on his face. The children looked up and noticed other vampires advancing on them, muttering about how they were going to destroy them. Tara grabbed Jonathan's father, who struggled against her grip, to no avail Jonathan ran around Tara and his father so fast that he was just a blur. The vampires started chasing him, but were soon chasing each other. Kelsey and Charlie crawled through the circle to get to Kelsey's father. Once they were in position, Jonathan started staking vampires. Tara held Jonathan's father and Kelsey and Charlie forced the potion down him. Once the last drop had been drunk and Jonathan had staked all 12 vampires, the children stood in a circle around their father and started reciting the spell.

"You shall be a vampire no more. You will be free from this hell."

A sudden roar stopped them in their tracks.

Thorn had woken up and was lunging at them. Kelsey screamed and Tara jumped up to fight him. Jonathan ran fast around Thorn and Tara, screaming to Kelsey and Charlie to finish the spell. As Jonathan grabbed the amulet from Thorn's neck, Thorn threw him into the wall.

"Oh no you don't!" Tara shouted as Thorn advanced on Jonathan. Flinging herself at him, she dragged him away from Jonathan.

"C'mon!" Charlie urged Kelsey, who was watching in horror.

Kelsey nodded, tears in her eyes and held Charlie's hands. They started the spell again.

"You will be a vampire no more. You will be free from this hell. To become human once again. We free you from this spell."

"Do you think it worked?" Kelsey whispered.

Charlie shrugged. "I dunno, but we need to get out of here!"

Tara was still fighting Thorn, but noticing the children had finished, she landed one final punch, knocking Thorn out again. Grabbing Jonathan and his father, they ran as fast as they could out of Thorn's lair, entering the deep, dark wood. Stopping for a few moments, Tara checked on Jonathan's head wound and strapped him up. Jonathan smiled at her gratefully.

"Come on!" he said, "we're not out of the woods yet." Everyone groaned at his pun, but hurried as fast as they could, until they saw a bright light. Looking at each other, they nodded and ran towards the light.

CHAPTER 19

BACK TO FAIRYLAND

The children, their father and Sparks landed in Fairyland in a heap.

"Children, you're back!" Gwendoline squealed in relief as she looked at the dirty, exhausted pile of limbs in front of her.

Once they were disentangled, the King and Queen greeted them. Jonathan looked nervously behind him.

"Don't worry, dear," the Queen spoke in a soft voice. "Thorn can't enter Fairyland. Our sun was created to be so that even Thorn can't enter without severe pain."

Jonathan nodded, relieved.

"Now, we feast!" The King boomed. The fairies cheered and set about making a feast fit for a King.

Once the table was decorated with all their favourite foods, the children sat down and ate greedily. There was every food they could imagine and it was all delicious. Kelsey kept dropping scraps to Sparks, who was lying contentedly under the table.

"Is that supposed to be doing that?" Tara pointed at her drink, which was shaking.

The King and Queen looked up and they all heard a terrifying roar and the rumbling got louder and louder.

"Earthquake!" Jonathan shouted.

"Not quite!" Thorn pushed into Fairyland. "It's amazing what potions you can get from your friend, Ash. After a little bit of torture, of course!" he smirked.

"If you've hurt him!" Jonathan shouted.

"You'll what?" Thorn sneered. "There is nothing you can do to me! Haven't you worked it out yet? You and your friends are worthless! You will never win!"

"You're wrong!" Tara shouted, grabbing Jonathan and dragging him to the hollow tree, followed by everyone else.

"We need to distract him whilst Kelsey puts the amulets in their places." Tara explained, looking back at Thorn advancing on them.

"What about me?" Charlie moaned. "I wanna help!"

"Charlie, you watch out for any more vampires, can you do that?" Charlie nodded proudly and ran to the edge of Fairyland.

Watching Charlie walk off, Jonathan and Tara nodded at each other and went to fight Thorn together.

Even through his calm exterior, Jonathan and Tara could see how furious Thorn was as he fought both of them. Tara looked at Jonathan. Thorn seemed stronger somehow and Jonathan looked in horror as Thorn grabbed Tara and threw her to one side. Watching Tara hit her head and fall unconscious, Jonathan screamed and lunged at Thorn. Thorn lunged back, but Jonathan dodged him and ran circles around Thorn.

Thorn stood perfectly still and suddenly thrust his arm out and grabbed Jonathan by the throat. Jonathan struggled but it was no use. Thorn grabbed Jonathan's sword and plunged it into Jonathan.

Kelsey screamed and Thorn turned her way, a hideous look on his face.

Kelsey started panicking; She'd only got 10 amulets in and Thorn was coming towards her.

"Keep going, Kelsey!" Gwendoline urged. "We'll hold him off!"

Kelsey nodded, terrified and watched as the fairies flew around Thorn, blasting magic at him. Taking a deep breath, she put in another amulet.

The fairies fluttered around Thorn, trying to confuse him, but he swatted them to one side.

Sparks lunged for Thorn, to give Kelsey more time, but Thorn was ready for him and shot magic out of his fingers at Sparks, causing him to slump to the ground.

He tried getting up a few times to save Kelsey, but he couldn't and eventually his eyes closed and he was still. Kelsey had tears streaming down her face as everyone she cared about was being struck down.

Thorn noticed this, grinning and turned to Charlie.

"No!" Kelsey screamed.

The King and Queen turned to Kelsey. "We must get the amulets in their places or everyone will die. You are our only hope now!"

Kelsey nodded resolutely and kept putting the amulets away.

She ignored the sounds of Charlie shouting, pellets from his sling shot at Thorn and the sickening thud of Charlie landing against the hollow tree.

Kelsey looked in horror at the last two amulets that needed to go in the tree. Thorn stalked towards Kelsey and went to grab her, but he heard a yell and he fell. He looked up and Kelsey's Dad had thrown himself at Thorn.

Kelsey didn't wait any longer and put the last two amulets in the tree.

The tree started glowing and Kelsey climbed down and stepped back. A sudden flash of light appeared and a cage of vines formed around Thorn, flinging Kelsey's Dad back.

"NOOOO!" Thorn roared.

The King and Queen stood next to the cage, reciting a spell, in an ancient language, to protect the cage.

Thorn threw himself at the vines and was instantly thrown back.

The rest of the fairies gathered around the cage and recited another spell.

Kelsey looked in amazement as the cage, and Thorn, disappeared. "Where's it gone?"

"It's gone to a barren wasteland where Thorn can't escape and no one goes." Gwendoline replied.

"Hooray! Thorn has gone. The warriors saved us!" The fairies all cheered.

Kelsey looked at everyone on the ground and started sobbing. "They've all gone!"

"Wait here!" Gwendoline ordered and hurried away when she came back, she was carrying a vial. "This is the elixir of life. One drop on their wounds and they will be healed."

"But they're not moving!" Kelsey cried.

"Trust me," Gwendoline urged.

Kelsey looked at Gwendoline and her friends and family. Nodding, she took the vial and went to Jonathan and poured one drop on his wound and waited.

Gwendoline coughed and pointed to the others, so Kelsey hurried and poured one drop on Tara's and Charlie's head wounds and poured the last drop onto the gash on Spark's lifeless body.

"Now we wait," Gwendoline said.

Kelsey didn't want to wait, but she did as she was told. It seemed like she'd been waiting for hours when she heard a groan from Jonathan. She squealed and ran to Jonathan, hugging him hard.

The others started sitting up and Kelsey hugged each of them in turn, even Charlie.

"Now, we can party!" The King boomed.

The fairies bustled around and soon there was music and fairy lights strung everywhere.

With the party in full swing, the children sought out the King and Queen and asked what would become of their father and explained what went wrong with the spell.

The King looked thoughtful for a moment and said, "I believe that your father is not completely cured." At the look of dismay on their faces, he continued, "However, I think he will be a human-vampire hybrid. He will probably be sensitive to the sun and start eating raw meat, but otherwise he should be back to normal."

The children heaved a sigh of relief.

"What about Ash?" Please can someone check on him?" Kelsey begged.

The King clicked his fingers and some fairies flew up to them. After a quick conversation, they flew away again.

"Not to worry," The Queen said kindly. "Those are our best medics and will do their best for Ash."

Jonathan still looked worried.

"What is it, child?" The Queen asked.

"We've been gone for ages and our mother will be furious!"

The Queen smirked. "No matter how long you are here, only a day has passed in the human world."

"What about Sparks?" Kelsey asked.

The Queen nodded to Gwendoline and Gwendoline shot some purple magic at Sparks. "Now, Sparks will look just like a dog from your world," Gwendoline explained. "You'll see him, but outsiders will just see a playful dog."

Kelsey hugged Gwendoline, or tried to as it was very difficult to hug someone the size of your thumb.

"We must say goodbye to you all now," the Queen said. "Thank you for everything you have done for us. We will not forget it."

The King nodded in agreement.

"We'll never forget you!" Kelsey cried as Gwendoline started guiding them back to the tree where it all started.

Standing next to the tree, Gwendoline said a tearful goodbye to the children and clapped her hands 3 times.

There was a flash of light and everyone covered their eyes. When they opened them, they were back in Jonathan's garden, wondering if that had all happened.

Sparks bounded up to them, licking them each in turn, leaving no doubt.

"Children!" Jonathan and Kelsey's mother called from inside the house. They all looked at each other and went in, wondering if they'd ever see their friends again.

Epilogue

6 months later

Kelsey and Charlie were playing with Sparks in the living room.

"Kelsey! Be careful!" her mum scolded for the 6th time.

"Sorry Mum!" Kelsey shouted, cheerfully.

"You know, it's funny," her mum continued. "Sometimes, when the dog jumps it almost seems like he is flying!" she shook her head and carried on with the housework. Kelsey and Charlie smirked at each other.

"Come on! Let's take Sparks in the garden!" Charlie suggested.

Kelsey thought it was a bit cold, in February, to be playing in the garden but she agreed it would be good for Sparks.

Getting their coats on, they ran into the garden with Sparks and started throwing snowballs at each other, which Sparks caught in his mouth.

"When do you think Tara and Jonathan will be back?" Charlie squealed as he narrowly dodged a snowball.

Kelsey shrugged, laughing. Jonathan and Tara had been dating for 6 months now and were practically inseparable. Kelsey thought it was a bit icky, but her brother was less grumpy, so she supposed it was a good thing.

"Kelsey! What are you doing out here? It's freezing!"

Kelsey rolled her eyes. Speak of the devil. "Hi Jon. We thought Sparks wanted some fresh air."

Jonathan laughed, good naturedly, and ruffled her hair.

Still holding Tara's hand, he said, "Let's go in…"

"Jonathan?" Tara looked at him quizzically.

"Shhh, I heard something!"

Jonathan and the others crept towards the bush, which appeared to be moving.

Jonathan peered in the bush and fell backwards as hundreds of tiny squeaking lights flew out of the bush.

The children all looked at each other, with growing excitement.

Here we go again…

About the Author

Sarah is 42 years old and lives in West Yorkshire, UK. She lives with her 3 kids and her dog and has enjoyed writing since she was a child.

Printed in the United States
by Baker & Taylor Publisher Services